#11

JUNIOR HIGH

THE GREAT
EIGHTH GRADE
SWITCH

JUNIOR HIGH

#11

JUNIOR HIGH

THE GREAT EIGHTH GRADE SWITCH

Kate Kenyon

SCHOLASTIC INC.
New York Toronto London Auckland Sydney

ISBN 0-590-41415-1

Copyright © 1988 by Ann Reit. All rights reserved. Published by Scholastic Inc. JUNIOR HIGH is a registered trademark of Scholastic Inc.

12 11 10 9 8 7 6 5 4 3 2 1   8 9/8 0 1 2 3/9

Printed in the U.S.A.   01

First Scholastic printing, July 1988

Chapter 1

The social studies room was quiet. Ms. Dalton, the pretty, young teacher, was talking in her usual low voice, and the students in the class were in various stages of drifting. No one was totally listening to what Ms. Dalton was saying.

Nora Ryan was staring at her best-friend-since-kindergarten's long, silky dark hair, thinking, Jen would look great if she'd cut her hair. Nora put her hand up to her own short, curly brown hair and pushed it away from her forehead. She knew that since she was going to be a doctor someday, she could never let her hair grow long. After all, what patient wants the doctor's hair hanging in the incision?

Jennifer Mann, unaware that Nora was restyling her hair, was bent over her own desk. She was trying to design a new button for the Save the Whales group she belonged to. The whale group was just one of the many useful activities in which Jen was involved. Jen cared deeply about everyone. Now, carefully, she wrote the letters STW in the center of a circle. She tried to draw little whales around the letters, until she felt a hand on her arm.

Tracy Douglas was peering at what Jen had written. Her long blonde hair was almost touching Jen's paper. "Who is he?" Tracy whispered.

"Who is who?" Jen whispered back.

"Who is the boy, STW?" Tracy asked.

Jen put her hand over her mouth to keep from laughing out loud.

"It's not a boy. It's a whale," Jen said.

Tracy shrugged. "You're weird sometimes, Jen."

Jen tried to focus her attention on Ms. Dalton, but she could hardly keep from giggling over Tracy's unfailing interest in boys, even imaginary ones.

Jen's eyes moved to Denise and Mia, who sat next to each other. No two girls could be so different. Denise's blonde hair was perfect, but then everything about Denise was perfect. Her eyes were the bluest, her figure the slimmest, her clothes the trendiest. It wasn't just because she was Denise Hendrix and her family was rich and owned Denise Cosmetics. Denise would have been perfect if she had lived in a broom closet. If you were going to enjoy having Denise as a friend, you just had to accept the fact that she always looked ready to be photographed for a fashion magazine.

Mia, on the other hand, was only perfect if you happened to like punk. The color of her hair changed daily, and that day it was a bright pink, standing up in starched spikes. She had a pink leather collar around her neck that matched the pink leather collar that her boyfriend Andy Warwick had around his neck.

Denise was pretending not to notice that almost every boy in the classroom was trying to get her attention, most of them not very subtly. But subtlety was not the strong point of most of the boys in the eighth grade. There wasn't one boy, except maybe Steve Crowley, who wouldn't have given almost anything to take Denise out, just once. Steve was more levelheaded than the rest of the boys, and would rather have been with Jen or Nora . . . but especially with Jen.

But Tommy Ryder, who thought every girl was crazy about him, or should be, and Mitch Pauley, who thought every girl was bowled over by his athletic ability, never gave up trying to interest Denise.

Jason Anthony didn't pay much attention to Denise, or any girl. Mostly because he knew that no girl like Denise would be attracted to him, with his bristly red hair and skinny body. As far as Jason was concerned, more important than any girl was his skateboard. The same skateboard that was the constant source of problems between him and every teacher in the school, and the principal, Mr. Donovan. Even now the skateboard was hidden under Jason's seat . . . except that everyone knew it was there.

Ms. Dalton looked at the eighth grade class and slowly picked up a stack of books and let them fall to the floor. The loud bang made everyone jump, and Susan Hillard, who was not known for her manners or her kindness, said spontaneously, "*What* did you *do?*"

Irene Dalton said casually, "Well, I *did* get everyone's attention. What's with all of you today? No one is here."

The class was silent, even Susan. How did you tell a teacher, especially one you liked, that you were bored?

Ms. Dalton tried again. "Come on. Someone let me in on what is going on. You know you can talk to me. I'm really on your side . . . most of the time." She smiled.

The class shifted nervously in their seats, and still no one said anything.

Ms. Dalton looked at Tracy. "Tracy, you're an honest girl. What is bothering you?"

Tracy was not able to pretend. She just always said things as they came into her head. "Well," she began, "I guess I'm just bored. Oh, not with you, Ms. Dalton. You're great . . . for a teacher . . . but I'm just bored with my own boring life."

Ms. Dalton looked around the room. "And you, Jen? Are you bored, too?"

Jen gave Tracy a disgusted look. Why did Tracy have to blurt out whatever came into her mind? Jen didn't want to hurt Ms. Dalton's feelings. It wasn't the teacher's fault that Jen wished life was more exciting.

"Jen, you're not answering me."

Jen squirmed in her seat. "I guess it's like Tracy said. It's not you . . . it's life. It's just so . . . predictable."

That should impress Steve . . . predictable.

"And you?" Ms. Dalton turned to Denise.

Denise glared at Jen. "Well, yes, I wish things were more interesting here . . . everywhere."

Ms. Dalton swept her arm around the classroom. "And the rest of you?"

First there was silence. Then everyone was talking at once.

"I always *know* I'm going to win the basketball game," Mitch said.

"That's what you call humility," Tommy

said under his breath. And then out loud, "But, of course, I guess I always know that girls are going to like me."

Mia hooted. "Not *this* girl. But that's every day, too. I know Tommy is going to be conceited, and I know I'm going to kid him about it."

"And you, Steve?" Ms. Dalton asked, turning to look at Steve Crowley.

Steve's face reddened. "Well, life is more interesting for me lately . . . because. . . ." He fastened his eyes on Jen's sleeve, not wanting to look right at her. But she knew what he meant. Her face reddened to match his.

"I didn't mean that *everything* was totally predictable," Jen blurted out. She didn't want Steve to think that their going out on a date was the usual, boring thing.

Ms. Dalton smiled. "I understand what you mean, Jen. And you Jason? What do you feel?"

"Does he have real feelings, too?" Tommy called out.

Jason ignored him and grinned his crazy grin. "Well, I'm just such an unusual-type guy that how could anyone in this class be bored?"

A groan went through the room.

"Oh, sure, Jason, you really make every day a joy," Susan said.

Ms. Dalton was silent. She sat at her desk and pushed a pencil back and forth. The class watched her, equally silent. Then Nora asked, "What are you thinking, Ms. Dalton?"

Irene Dalton looked around the room. Her eyes rested on almost every student before moving on to the next one. Finally she said slowly, "I have an idea. An experiment that would be very interesting and maybe teach you a lot."

"Something *else* to teach us a lot?" Andy Warwick asked. "My head is stuffed already."

"So hang it over a mantelpiece," Tommy shouted, and then broke up.

Ms. Dalton stood up and began walking around the room. "Suppose, just suppose, you could all change places for a week. You could live in each other's homes and follow the pattern of another person's life."

"How would we do it?" Nora asked, always the practical scientist.

"I think the best thing to do," Ms. Dalton said, "is to put everyone's name into a hat. Then you will each pull out a name and that's whose home you'll be in for a week."

"What if I pull out my own name?" Jason asked plaintively.

"What if I get your name?" Andy asked in mock terror. "What luck."

"If we don't like the name we pull, can we change it for another one?" Jen asked, her concern easily heard in her voice.

Ms. Dalton shook her head, "No, Jen. You get one draw, and you're stuck with what you pull the first time."

The class was silent again, and then they started yelling.

"I want to be at Denise's house!" Mitch shouted.

"Yeah," Tommy answered, "but she won't be there."

"It's great," Lucy Armanson said. "I love it."

"When do we start?" Tracy asked.

"Hold on," Ms. Dalton said. "This is something that is going to take a little time to work out. First, we have to get the approval of the school. Then, everyone who participates has to get their parents' approval. Then, if that all works out, the Great Eighth Grade Switch will begin."

The bell rang, and Ms. Dalton called over the class's loud voices, "I'll talk to Mr. Donovan right now. I have a free period. Meet me in this room after your last period, and I'll let you know what he says."

The day dragged on for the eighth grade social studies class. They could hardly wait to hear what Mr. Donovan had decided. When the group gathered together again at the end of the day, the smile on Ms. Dalton's face gave away the answer.

"My new life begins," Mitch said.

"Wait," Irene Dalton said firmly. "You have to get unqualified approval from your parents. They will have to sign a paper, and you will have to sign it, too. You will have to agree to live up to all the rules that will be laid down by the school. Now, I had forms made up for you to take home to your parents. Have them read the forms very carefully. There will be a meeting here tomorrow night at eight o'clock for all you kids who are going to take part in this, your parents, and some of the school faculty. Tell your parents that any questions they have will be answered then."

The eighth-graders spilled out of the school, hardly able to believe what they considered to be their good luck. Jen and Nora walked home together, as usual.

"Okay, Jen, I know what that funny look on your face means. You're worried about something. What?"

Jen kicked at a pebble in the street and pushed her long dark hair off her face. "I don't know. I guess I'm a little scared."

Nora stopped walking and took Jen's arm. "Scared of what?"

Jen shrugged. "What if I don't like the name I pull out of the hat?"

Nora laughed and began walking again.

"Jen, you're not moving in forever. It's only for a week."

But Jen wasn't satisfied. "What if the family I pick doesn't like me?"

"That's dumb, Jen. Who wouldn't like you?"

Jen smiled at Nora's wholehearted acceptance of her. No one could be a better friend than Nora. "Well, *someone* might not like me. I know I get very intense and stubborn sometimes."

"So," Nora answered, "for one week, loosen up. Be cool."

Jen ignored Nora. "I don't even know if my father will let me do it. Since my mother died, he's kind of, well, I guess, overprotective."

"Well, get Jeff to work on your father," Nora said.

Jen shook her head. "Jeff is one of the family in most things, but he is still officially the housekeeper. I don't know if my dad will listen to Jeff in something as important as this."

"Jen," Nora said threateningly, "you know you can get your father to let you do anything you want to do that doesn't endanger life and limb. Just smile and tilt your head in that little-girl way you do. Your father will be a pushover. But you have to really try hard."

"I'll try. I'll try," Jen said.

"Listen," Nora said, "he lets you eat white bread and candy bars that don't have anything real in them. So he'll let you do this."

Jen laughed at Nora's distaste for any food that didn't seem one hundred percent natural to her. "I hope you have to live in a house where they have never heard of granola or alfalfa sprouts. That will change your health food kick."

Nora paled a little. "That's a possibility, isn't it? What would I do?"

"You'll just have to loosen up and be cool," Jen said, laughing.

Chapter 2

Jen waited until the family was around the dining room table to bring up the subject of the Eighth Grade Switch. Jeff had just brought in a platter of hamburgers made just the way Jen loved them, with a thick tomato sauce over them. She put one patty on her plate and then just stared at it.

"Jen, what's wrong?" her father asked. "You're not eating."

Jen cleared her throat and said, "Well, there's something I want to talk to you about . . . something important."

"You failed a subject in school," Eric, Jen's younger brother, said hopefully. "Great. You're not perfect after all."

"I didn't fail anything," Jen said indignantly.

"Nuts," Eric muttered.

"Come on, Jen, what's on your mind?" Jeff asked, cutting into his hamburger.

"Well," Jen began, "we are going to have this experiment in social studies. We're all going to pull names out of a hat and go live in that name's house for a week."

Ted Mann held his hand up. "Wait! Just a minute! Let me try to understand this. *You* are going to live in some other child's house for a week? You won't be in your own home, where you belong?"

"I knew it," Jen murmured to herself.

Jeff looked at Jen piercingly from under his bushy gray eyebrows. His blue eyes never left Jen's face. "What's the point of this experiment, Jen?"

Jen sighed. "Well, everyone in Ms. Dalton's class admitted they were bored. So she, Ms. Dalton, said she thought we'd learn a lot if we just changed places with another kid."

"That may be," Jen's father said, "but what kid? I can't let you go just anywhere."

"Ted," Jeff Crawford said, "we know every kid in Jen's class. They are all nice."

"But what about their parents? We don't know all of them, do we?"

"Let her go, Dad. Think how great it would be to have her away for a week," Eric said.

"Thanks a bunch, Eric. You really are

a love of a brother," Jen said, sticking out her tongue at Eric.

Jeff was thoughtful. Then he said, "No, I don't know all the parents and neither do you, but — "

"Dad," Jen interrupted. "There's going to be a meeting tomorrow night, and you can ask all the questions you have, then. Ms. Dalton will be there, and the other parents, and some faculty, too. Just don't say no yet. *Please.*"

Ted Mann looked at Jen and then said, "Okay. I'll go to the meeting, and Jeff will come, too, and then we'll decide."

Jen let out a breath. At least there was a chance she could be part of the Great Eighth Grade Switch.

Denise was sitting on the edge of her bed in her pink, plum, and white bedroom. Her mother was picking up the clothes Denise had just taken off and dropped on the floor.

"You mean you are going to go to any kid's house you pick out of a hat?" Denise's mother asked with wide eyes.

"Yes! What's wrong with that?" Denise asked defiantly.

Ms. Hendrix laughed and sat down next to Denise. "Wrong? Nothing is wrong . . . I think it's wonderful. I can't wait to see you picking up your own clothes. Doing your own laundry. Helping with the dishes. I just can't wait."

Denise looked concerned. "I never thought about that. Maybe I just changed my mind."

"Oh, no!" Ms. Hendrix said. "We are going to be at that meeting tomorrow night and sitting in the first row. I love it!"

Nora Ryan was scraping the leftovers on a dish into the garbage pail. "So you see," she said to her mother, who was filling the dishwasher, and to her father, who was drying the pots, "it should be an extremely valuable experience for all of us. It will teach us how to . . . how to. . . ." How to what? Nora thought.

"Yes?" Jessica Ryan said, straightening up from the dishwasher. "How to what?"

"How to eat something filled with additives just once in a while," Mr. Ryan said.

"You sound just like Jen," Nora said, laughing.

"Why do you want her to eat food filled with additives?" Ms. Ryan asked her husband.

"Not often," he answered. "Just once in a while, like a normal kid. Is that wrong?"

Nora's older sister Sally walked into the kitchen at that moment and said, "You're perfectly right, Dad. We have to humanize Nora a little."

"You want to be a dancer someday," Nora said accusingly to Sally. "Well, you just better watch what you eat. You know dancers are very careful about what they put into their systems and you . . . *you* are a human garbage pail."

"Okay! Okay, girls," Ms. Ryan said. "I know all the kids and all their parents, and I think it would be good for Nora. It will . . . well, loosen her up a little."

"Wait a minute," Nora said, "Who said I needed loosening?"

"I did," Sally said.

"Well, you don't know anything." Nora fought back.

"Can we all just stop arguing?" Nora's mother asked. "Let your father give his opinion."

"Well," Mr. Ryan said to his wife, "if you think it's okay, I'll go along with that. But I want to go to that meeting tomorrow night."

Nora ran over to her mother and hugged her. "Thanks, Mom. You're super."

"I've noticed," Jessica Ryan said, "that I'm only super when I do what you want."

Later that night, Nora dialed Jen's number, as she did every night, and waited for Jen's breathless voice.

"Hi," Jen said.

"So how did it go?" Nora asked.

Jen cradled the pink princess phone under her chin and picked at the white chenille bedspread on her bed. "Well, Dad didn't say no, but he didn't say yes, either. He and Jeff are coming to the meeting tomorrow night. Then they'll decide. I think Jeff feels it's okay. It's my father who's the problem. What about you?"

"It's okay for me. But my folks are coming tomorrow night, too," Nora said. "Don't worry, Jen. I'll get my mother to talk to your father and she'll convince him it's okay. I know it."

Jen stared at the ceiling of her room. "I hope so. But I'm not so sure. My father can be very stubborn."

"So that's where you get it from," Nora said.

"What are you going to wear tomorrow?" Jen asked, ignoring Nora's last remark.

They had gone through that ritual for as long as they could remember. Each night they would call each other, and before the conversation was over they would decide what they were going to wear to school the next day.

Nora thought for a while. "It's going to be cool tomorrow. So, I guess my red-and-white striped sweater and my navy skirt with red tights."

"I like it," Jen said. "Okay, I guess I'll

wear my light-blue jeans and that yellow sweater Dad gave me for my last birthday."

"Good," Nora said. "That yellow sweater is great with your dark hair. I wish I could let my hair grow, but I was just thinking this morning that my patients might not like it."

"Nora," Jen said slowly, "you're not going to have any patients for a hundred years. You could grow your hair and cut it fifty times before you'll have your first patient."

"Time flies," Nora answered.

"You're nuts," Jen replied. "Good-night, Nora."

Before she went to sleep, Jen took out her diary and wrote:

I guess I really want to be part of the Switch, but I am also very nervous about it. I've never lived in a strange place for a week. And I don't know how good I'll be at it. Maybe I'll just get so homesick, I'll have to go home. I mean, that would really disgrace me.

I wish Gramma was here. It's funny, when she came to visit from England just a little while ago, I was so annoyed at her so much of the time. She seemed so bossy and cold, and I thought she liked Nora too much. But if it hadn't been for her, I might never have gone out with Steve on a real date.

Now I think if she were here, she could help me feel a little braver about this Eighth Grade Switch thing. I don't have time to write her and get an answer back. I guess I just have to be brave on my own.

Steve Crowley was in the kitchen of his father's restaurant, washing lettuce for the salads. He held the leaves under the running water and thought about Jen. Supposing he pulled her name out of the hat? If he had to live with Jeff Crawford, he knew Jeff would guess that Steve liked, really liked, Jen. Not just as a since-kindergarten friend, but as a girl. Jeff saw everything. Maybe, Steve thought, it was living to be fifty, like Jeff, that made you smart. But Steve wasn't ready to talk about what he felt for Jen with anyone yet. It was all so new. One minute Jen was just good old Jen, and the next she was Jen with long, silky hair and big hazel eyes that made his heart pump harder. He just couldn't figure out how it happened.

"Steve," a voice boomed. "How clean do you think lettuce has to be?"

Steve turned and looked into his father's gray eyes. "I was dreaming, Dad. Sorry."

"Dream later, Stevie-boy. After the customers leave."

Suddenly Steve remembered. "Later, I have to talk to you about something important. It's crucial, Dad. I have to ask you something."

Mr. Crowley took the lid off of a steaming pot and glanced into the boiling potatoes. "What's so important?"

"It's switching homes. The eighth grade is going to have an experiment. We're going to live in each other's homes for a week."

A waiter came racing into the kitchen. "Table four is going to leave unless they get their food right now."

Steve shouted above the waiter's voice. "Can I do it, Dad?"

"Do what?" Mr. Crowley asked distractedly.

"Be part of the Eighth Grade Switch."

"Can you still help out here?" Mr. Crowley asked.

"Sure," Steve answered quickly.

"Then I don't care how many kids' houses you switch with," his father said, pouring the water off the potatoes.

"Thanks, Dad." Steve grinned, knowing that later on, when his father thought about what he had said, he'd be the first one at the meeting the next night.

Mia was in her bathroom, emptying the medicine chest into a rubber-lined cosmetic bag. She looked at each bottle, jar, and tube and then added it to the contents of the bag.

Mrs. Stevens came into the bathroom and watched for a minute. "You're throwing all that out?" Mia's mother asked, hope flooding her voice. "You're going to let your hair be a real color? Aren't you?"

Mia frowned. "Of course not. I'm just packing."

"Packing for *what?*"

Quickly, Mia filled her mother in on the details of the Eighth Grade Switch.

"Maybe you'll get to live at Lucy's," Mrs. Stevens said, "and you'll look wonderful, like she does . . . with real clothes and real hair. Wouldn't you like that?" Mrs. Stevens was almost begging Mia to say yes.

"You mean I can be part of the experiment then?" Mia asked eagerly.

"Wait a minute!" her mother said. "We have to talk more about this. I'd like your hair to look like hair, but I have to know more about this whole thing."

Mia sighed. "Okay, come tomorrow night."

Jason was polishing his skateboard when his father took it out of his hands.

"Don't you have homework . . . or something?"

"I did it already." Jason reached for the skateboard.

"Jason, don't you think you're too old for this?" his father asked.

"Well, I could devote more time to girls," Jason said slyly. But thinking about his recent experience with Monique Gorgée, the French exchange student, he was just as glad not to be involved with girls. Moni had really liked him, and Jason had found this hard to cope with. Now they were just friends and that was fine with Jason.

"Okay! Okay!" Mr. Anthony handed the skateboard back to Jason.

"I'm going away for a few days," Jason said casually.

Mr. Anthony looked suspicious, "Away *where*?"

Again, as had happened all over Cedar Groves, the details of the Eighth Grade Switch were sketched out.

Mr. Anthony thought a few minutes. "Will you leave the skateboard at home?"

Jason looked astounded. "Of course not. Would you go on a trip without your *car*?"

"Jason, a car is not the same thing as a skateboard."

Jason looked superior. "Wheels are wheels."

Mr. Anthony looked at Jason with disbelief. Then he asked, "Is everyone part of this switch thing? I mean Tommy and

Mitch and Steve? Are their parents letting them go?"

"Sure. Of course," Jason answered with confidence.

"How do you know?" his father asked. "Have you spoken to them?"

"Well, not quite," Jason admitted. "There's a meeting tomorrow night. Come and you'll see. I'm sure their parents will let them go."

"We'll see tomorrow night," Mr. Anthony said.

Chapter 3

The eighth grade gathered on the steps of the school the next morning. It was almost cold, but no one would dare go inside. It wouldn't have been cool to set one foot through the door before the bell rang. So the class huddled together, making small talk until they heard the bell.

That morning all they talked about was the Eighth Grade Switch.

"It's the best thing that ever happened to us," Tracy said with assurance.

"How would you know?" Susan asked in her usual sarcastic tone.

Tracy looked hurt and Jen came to her rescue. "Susan, try to be nice. Just for once. Tracy knows a good thing when she sees it."

"Yeah," Tracy agreed. "Like him." She wagged her head in the direction of a boy with dark brown hair, who was walking up the steps toward Jen.

Jen wanted to say something to Tracy. Something like . . . Go flirt with some other boy. But she couldn't. She didn't have to anyway, because Steve Crowley didn't look at Tracy. He came up to Jen and smiled. "Hi," he said.

Jen thought she had never heard anyone say "Hi," with as much style as Steve.

"Hi," Jen replied. That's a brilliant piece of conversation, Jen thought.

"This brilliant conversation is too much for me," Susan said and walked away.

I can't argue with her about that, Jen thought.

"I don't think that was so brilliant," Tracy said, seriously. "All they did was say 'Hi.' What's so great about that?"

Susan looked at Tracy over her shoulder. "You're too much."

"What did your father say about the switch?" Steve asked Jen.

Jen shrugged. "You know my father. He's coming to the meeting tonight with Jeff. Then he'll come to the great decision. What did your father say?"

"He said it was okay. But I know he's going to have second thoughts."

Nora joined them, wrapping her scarf tighter around her neck. "My mother thinks it's a great idea and my father hopes I'll have to eat things with BHT and artificial colors in them."

"Well, my mother hopes I'll have to clean my own room," Denise said, brushing her gleaming blonde hair back from her face. Little silver earrings glistened in her ears, matching the narrow silver bracelets around her wrists. She wore a cowl-necked, soft, pink angora sweater and tight black pants, and, as always, she looked like she had walked off the pages of *Seventeen*.

Mia Stevens looked away from the small mirror she held, which reflected the spiky hair that was green this morning. "My mother is hoping I'll get to live at Lucy's and come back home a lady. She's in for a big surprise."

At eight that night, one of the larger classrooms was jammed with people. The entire eighth grade social studies class was there with their parents. Ms. Dalton was sitting at the desk in the front of the room. Seated on chairs next to her were Mr. Donovan; Mrs. Carpenter, the school secretary, ready to take notes; Cliff Rochester, the English teacher all the girls had once had a crush on; Ms. Hogan, the drama teacher, who was sure there was a play in the idea of an eighth grade switch; and Mr. Armand, the French teacher, who was going to organize the project with Ms. Dalton.

The noise in the room was deafening, as

the students were making last-minute attempts to get their parents to give them an unqualified yes. Their parents were mostly yelling at them to keep quiet. Ms. Dalton was banging on her desk with a gavel, trying to get everybody's attention. But the sound of the gavel was lost in the general chaos in the room. Finally, Nora's mother stood up, put her fingers into her mouth, and gave a piercing whistle. The room was suddenly totally silent, and chic, pretty Jessica Ryan sat down, smiling with satisfaction.

"*Moth-er*," Nora said, looking around. "Do you have to make a spectacle of yourself?"

"Nora," Mrs. Ryan answered, "I have to get home sometime tonight to read some papers for a case I'm trying tomorrow. I'm sorry if I didn't live up to your idea of the perfect mother, but life will go on."

"Thank you, Mrs. Ryan," Irene Dalton said with appreciation. "Now let's try to get things going. As you all know, we would like, that is the eighth-graders and I would like, to perform a little experiment. Our idea is to see what would happen if the kids switched homes for one week. They would live in the appointed home, obeying all the rules of that home, following all the routines, eating the food, joining in the running of the house, and so on. They would come to school every day as usual, and after school would do whatever their substitute parents felt were the proper things for them to do. The one weekend involved would be spent the same way . . . and then on Sunday afternoon they would return to their real homes. We would then spend a number of periods discussing what was learned, and the students will write a paper on their experience."

"Wait a minute, Ms. Dalton," Mitch Pauley yelled. "You never mentioned a paper before now."

"Didn't I?" Ms. Dalton asked innocently. "Well, I must have forgotten. Of course, I know you won't mind writing a short paper, so that your parents can all share in what you learned from your week away from home."

"I think we've been had," Tommy said under his breath.

"Don't be ridiculous," Nora said. "What's a little paper?"

"She's right," Denise added. "It will be worth it."

Mr. Mann stood up and waved at Ms. Dalton. "I have a number of questions."

The teacher nodded. "I'm sure many people have. Let's just get them all out and we can talk them over."

"Okay." Ted Mann cleared his throat.

"Now, I'm not an overprotective father. . . ."

Jen rolled her eyes upward and Nora giggled.

Mr. Mann gave Jen a *don't-say-a-word* look and went on. "As I was saying, I'm not an overprotective father, but after all, I can't just let my daughter go off anywhere. It isn't that I don't trust all of you, but. . . ."

Jen put her head in her hands and let her long hair fall over her face.

Ms. Dalton stood up and smiled at Mr. Mann. "I'm sure all the parents in this room sympathize with your feelings."

There were murmuring sounds of agreement.

"But," Ms. Dalton went on, "you all know each other fairly well. Everyone is reliable, and the people that Jen ends up living with for a week will, I'm sure, be able to reassure you in any way you need."

"Well," Ted Mann said, hesitating, "I might be a little stricter with Jen than some parents would be. I mean, since her mother died. . . ."

Jen moaned softly. *"I'm* going to die," she said to Nora.

"It's not as bad as having a mother who whistles like a six-year-old," Nora whispered back.

"Actually," Ted Mann said, "I don't know everyone in this room. I mean, I can't look around and feel that it's okay for Jen to live with that person or this one. No offense to anyone."

"Don't you worry, Mr. Mann," a loud voice said. "I'll look after Jen." Steve Crowley grinned and looked very pleased with himself.

Jen stared at Steve and then said, "Please, I don't need anyone to take care of me. What's wrong with you two? I'm not a helpless child."

Steve blushed and looked down at his hands.

"Now you've done it," Nora whispered. "You've hurt his male ego."

Jen looked over at Steve. "I appreciate your concern for me, Steve, but really, I *can* look after myself."

Steve smiled. "Sorry, Jen. You're right." Then he winked at Mr. Mann.

"Boys!" Jen muttered.

Irene Dalton rapped the gavel. "I think we are getting off the track," she said.

Jessica Ryan stood up. "I think whoever gets Nora should know that she eats rather strangely."

"What does that mean?" Barbara Hendrix asked. "My cook is French, and she doesn't like people not eating what she prepares."

Denise tugged at her mother's arm. "Mother, don't make a fuss. If we get Nora, she'll eat what Mimi makes."

"Now wait a minute!" Nora shouted. "Not if it's high in cholesterol."

Mrs. Hendrix pushed Denise's hand off her arm. "High in cholesterol? Mimi doesn't know how to make anything that doesn't have cream and butter in it."

Nora turned to her mother. "Mother! I can't eat that kind of stuff."

Steve Crowley's father stood up. "And I need Steve in the restaurant in the afternoons."

Mrs. Stevens shouted, "Somebody will have to do something about Mia's hair."

Ms. Dalton pushed her own hair off her forehead. "Mrs. Stevens! Wherever Mia goes, it isn't going to be a beauty school."

Jason Anthony's father yelled, "Okay, who has a good fireplace that will accommodate one skateboard when the fire is roaring?"

"*I'm* not going to be part of this," Jason said, clutching his skateboard.

Suddenly, everyone was yelling at once. No one was listening to any voice but his or her own.

Nora was telling her mother how much she had embarrassed her. Jen was begging her father to be reasonable. Steve was shouting that he wasn't sure he could be at the restaurant every day. And everybody else was either shouting at a parent or the parents were shouting at each other.

Suddenly, Mr. Donovan stood up and yelled *"Quiet!"*

Irene Dalton's wide blue eyes narrowed and she said in a steely voice, "Thank you, Mr. Donovan. I will take over now."

She pressed her hands together and looked out over her silent audience. First she looked, one by one, at the students. "Do you kids want to do this switch or not?" she asked.

A loud *"Yes"* went through the room.

"Okay," the teacher went on, "then you have to stop all this nonsense about what you'll eat, or how you'll do your hair, or what you do with your toys." At the last word she looked at Jason.

"This is no *toy*," Jason said, hugging the skateboard.

"Jas, shut up!" Nora said.

Then, Ms. Dalton let her eyes move over the parents. "And you parents have to be more reasonable, too. Your kids are not in kindergarten. They are eighth-graders and on their way to maturity. I am suggesting one week in a perfectly fine home. They aren't going white-water rafting, or joining a cult, or moving to Europe. They will all be very near you, and the school will keep a close eye on what they are doing. So if you want your child to be part of what could be a learning experience for them that might be important, you just all have to relax."

The room was silent.

"You all have release forms," Ms. Dalton continued. "If you don't have one, there are some on this desk. If you agree that your child can be part of this experiment, just sign the form. But I encourage you to decide now, so that we can continue."

Jessica Ryan took the form out of her pocketbook and signed it. Then she turned to Ted Mann. "Sign it, Ted. It will do you a lot of good."

"What about Jen?" Mr. Mann asked.

"Jen is fine. You need this more than she does."

Mr. Mann laughed. "I guess you're right. What do you think, Jeff?" He looked at Jeff Crawford.

"Sign it, Ted. Let her go," Jeff said, smiling.

Ted Mann looked at Jen. At her big, pleading eyes. "Okay." He signed with a flourish.

Jen threw her arms around her father. "Dad, thanks!"

Nora and Jen hugged each other and danced around the crowded room as well as they could manage.

One by one, the other parents signed.

Steve's father said, "I guess I can get along at the restaurant without you for a week."

Mrs. Stevens signed, muttering, "I still hope somebody does something about her hair."

Denise's mother took a silver pen out of her bag and signed. "Somebody make her hang up her clothes. Please."

The room was a mass of parents signing forms, students hugging each other, and endless jokes about where they would end up. Jeff came over to Jen and put his arms around her. "Well, we did it!" he said. "He's really going to let you go."

Jen kissed Jeff and rubbed her cheek against his. She could remember so clearly the day Jeff arrived at the Mann household. A lot of people thought it was strange that the Manns had a male housekeeper, but after a succession of people who all had been totally unsatisfactory, Jeff had come and immediately fit into the family. He was a pal to Eric, someone Jen could always talk to, a wonderful cook, and a man whom Ted Mann would take advice from. Jen's one fear was that Jeff would someday marry his girlfriend Debby Kincaid, and leave them. But Nora would say not to look for trouble and that maybe by that time Jen herself might be grown-up and out of the house.

Everyone started to leave the classroom,

and over the noise of chairs being pushed back and people yelling good-night, Ms. Dalton shouted, "Kids, read your rules very carefully tonight. We'll talk about them tomorrow."

Chapter 4

The Manns and the Crowleys and the Ryans went to Temptations after the meeting to have something to eat and talk about the Great Switch. They sat around a large table, and Jen noticed that Steve made sure he was sitting next to her. Nora noticed, too, and raised her eyebrows. If she says one word, Jen thought, I'll kill her later. But Nora just kicked Jen under the table and didn't say anything.

"I'm still not sure about this," Ted Mann said.

Jessica Ryan sighed and said, "Ted, someday Jen is going to go off to college, or go on a dig in Israel, or run off and join the circus, or something. This will just prepare you for the big departure."

"Very funny," Mr. Mann said, frowning at Jessica Ryan.

"Okay," Jeff said as he read the menu. "What is everyone having?"

"I'll have the yogurt with fresh fruit," Nora said.

"Nora, can't you relax just tonight? Celebrate," Jen said.

"I am celebrating," Nora said. "I'm having the fruit, aren't I? That's *very* sweet."

"What are you having, Jen?" Steve asked.

Jen closed the menu and said defiantly, "I'll have the banana split with extra whipped cream."

Nora groaned. "I don't believe you."

Steve said, "I'll have the same."

He gave Jen a quick look and smiled. Jen thought he had the sweetest smile in the world.

Everyone gave the waitress their order and then Jeff asked, "What are the kids' rules that Ms. Dalton was talking about?"

Jen fished in her bag. "I have a copy of them here. Wait, I'll pull them out."

Carefully she emptied the huge bag while everyone at the table looked on in amazement. There was colorless nail polish; a makeup bag; ten buttons advising people to recycle paper, save the whales, not make unnecessary noise, not litter, not abandon animals, and other things of that sort. There was Kleenex; four pencils and three ballpoint pens; a wallet; a small address book; sunglasses; a flashlight; keys; a candy bar, mashed and stale;

chewing gum; a large hair brush; and a tube of toothpaste.

"Oh, here it is," Jen said, as she pulled out a sheet of instructions.

"Jen," her father asked, "do you carry all that stuff around all the time?"

"What stuff?" Jen asked.

"Never mind, Jen," Jeff said. "What are the rules?"

"Okay," Jen said, clearing her throat.

"One: You must obey all the rules of the house you will be living in. Two: You must treat your surrogate parents with respect. Three: You must call home every day. Four: You must come to school every day and follow your regular school routine. Five: You must remain in your surrogate home for the full week, unless there is some kind of emergency in your real home. Six: You must not confide any intimate things you find out about your new home to anyone, not even your best friend. Seven: You must not gossip to your surrogate parents about your own home. Eight: You must only bring the possessions that you will need for the week, and not clutter up the surrogate home. Nine: You must not borrow money from anyone in your surrogate home. Ten: You must be prepared to write a paper on your week when it is over."

Everyone was silent for a minute. Then

Mr. Crowley said, "Well, those seem like sensible rules to me. And not too hard for you kids to follow."

"What kind of intimate things do you suppose we'll find out about our new parents?" Nora asked, her eyes shining.

"Who knows?" Steve said. "But it could be *very* interesting."

"I like the fact that the kids have to phone home every day the best," Ted Mann said. He turned to Jen. "And don't forget it, either."

"I can't wait until tomorrow," Jen said. "Just think, I'll be a totally different person in someone else's house."

"What do you mean 'different'?" Jen's father asked, his voice filled with concern.

"Relax, Ted," Jeff said. "Jen is Jen, no matter what."

Nora looked at Jen with impatience. "What makes you think you're going to be totally different? What's going to be different?"

"I don't know," Jen said with annoyance. "I make an innocent statement and everyone is jumping all over me."

Jen felt Steve's hand on hers under the table. "I don't think you should be any different at all, Jen."

Jen smiled at Steve and once again thought how good-looking he was.

"Well," Nora said. "I wouldn't go that far, Steve. I mean, no one is perfect. Not even Jen."

Their orders came, and Nora shook her head as she looked at the huge banana split, topped with mounds of whipped cream, sitting in front of Jen.

Steve said to Jen, "Would you like some of my whipped cream? I know you like it a lot."

Jessica Ryan and Ted Mann exchanged a look and smiled at each other.

"Steve, she has enough whipped cream now to float a bakery," Mr. Mann said.

"She has enough whipped cream now to take care of her cholesterol allowance for the next decade," Nora said.

"So you take some, Nora," her mother said. "You can mix it in with the yogurt. You'll be starting a new taste sensation."

"Why is everyone so involved with what I eat?" Nora asked.

"Why are you so involved with what *I* eat?" Jen asked.

Jessica Ryan took out her wallet and said, "I think everyone is getting a little edgy. Let's eat up and get home. And this little party is on me."

"I'll have to get Debby to do that more often," Jeff said.

"I've seen Debby pay for you a lot," Jen said.

"I just like to complain a little," Jeff answered, laughing.

Later that night, when Jen was in bed, cuddled under her pink comforter, she remembered how warm Steve's hand had felt on hers. It was funny, but she hadn't even been embarrassed, or worried that her father might realize that Steve was holding her hand under the table. It just felt right. Everything about being with Steve felt right.

Jen leaned over and pushed some books aside on the night table next to her bed. She pulled her blue leather diary out from under the books and opened it to an entry she had written on a Sunday night a few weeks before. She had written it after her big date with Steve. Now she fluffed up her pillows and read:

Dear Diary:

I guess this has been a perfect night. Steve looked so handsome when he called for me, and he even brought me one red rose. I cut off the long stem. I guess that's kind of not chic to do, but how else could I pin it to my coat? I could see my father sort of go pale when I snipped off the stem. Later, he told me that I had been given a long-stemmed American Beauty rose, which was very special. Well, so I'm not up on what length stems should be.

Anyway, a waiter in Steve's father's restaruant drove us to the school. Mr. Crowley couldn't leave the restaurant. We went into the auditorium, where the play was going to be given. We were sort of doubling with Nora and Brad, but our seats weren't together. Is it disloyal to Nora to say I was glad? I mean I was glad we were doubling, but I liked being alone (with two hundred other kids) with Steve for a little while. When the lights went down and the play started, I have to admit I was much more aware of Steve than what was going on on the stage. But I think Steve was, too, more aware of me than the stage, I mean. Because not much later he took my hand and held it. He held it just right. Not too tight and not all limp and wimpy.

After the play we found Nora and Brad and we went for a pizza. We clowned around a lot about what to put on the pizza and who got to decide, the guys or the girls. The girls did. I think that's okay. Next time, if there is a next time, the guys will get their choice. Then Brad called his father, and he came and picked us up. I just keep thinking how wonderful it will be when someone is old enough to drive. You go on a date, which is a fairly grown-up thing to be doing, and then you have to get somebody's father or mother to come and cart you home. It makes you feel like a child. Mr. Hartley dropped Steve and me at my house, and Steve told him right away not to wait for him, that he could easily walk home from my house.

I knew. I really knew . . . and I was nervous. We stood in front of my house and talked a little. Steve kept shuffling his feet and then he did it. He leaned over and kissed me. I've been kissed once or twice at parties, when I was just a kid. But they were dumb kisses. I mean quick and awkward and lots of bumping noses and the guy always ran off afterward. But this was different. This was . . . I guess you'd say meaningful. And it wasn't awkward at all, and Steve didn't run away. He stood there, holding my hand. And then he said, "Jen, you know I never realized it before recently, but you are real beautiful."

That was a first for me. No boy had ever told me I was beautiful. My father has, but he doesn't count. "Steve, do you mean it?" I asked. That was dumb I guess, but I just wanted to make sure he wasn't just being polite.

"I mean it," he said.

Then he kissed me again, very sweetly, and he left.

I guess I love him.

Chapter 5

The steps of Cedar Groves Junior High were filled the next morning . . . but that was not unusual. But something *was* different. There was a division among the students that was unusual. The students who were going to be part of the Great Eighth Grade Switch were all together, laughing, playfully pushing each other around, hopping from foot to foot. The students who were not going to be part of the switch were watching them, talking among themselves, most of them wishing they, too, could be part of the Switch. Some of them hadn't gotten their parents' approval, some were nervous about the whole idea, and some weren't in Ms. Dalton's class. Even some of the high school crowd, who had heard about the experiment, had come over to the junior high just to watch whatever was going on.

Tony Hendrix, Denise's older brother,

whom Jen had once had a terrible crush on, was standing on a step below Jen.

"Hey, Jen. Hear you're going to change your life-style."

Jen laughed. "I guess. Not too much, I hope," she added quickly.

Tracy looked at Tony and narrowed her eyes in what she thought was a mature look. "I'd change my life-style for you any day, Tony," she said softly.

Susan Hillard made a gagging sound. "I can't stand this."

Mia stopped brushing her hair, which was blue that day, and made a face at Susan. "I feel sorry for the home that gets you for a week."

Susan glanced at Mia with a superior look. "At least I look like a human being, unlike some people I know."

Jason snickered. "Depends what you consider human."

Nora shook her head with annoyance. "Here we are, on one of the most important days of our lives, and you're all bickering and acting like children. Don't any of you have any sense of the monumental experience we are about to embark on?"

"I don't know if I'm ready for any monumental experiences," Mitch said.

"How monumental can it be?" Tommy asked. "I mean, one home is just like another. Isn't it? Really?"

"NO!" everyone yelled at once.

Just then the bell rang and the eighth grade piled into the halls of the school. Jason looked around quickly and then careened down the corridor on his skateboard.

"He'll never change," Nora whispered to Jen.

The social studies class was first period. If it hadn't been, Nora thought she wouldn't have survived the day. They all pushed each other into the classroom and sat in their usual seats, but they were all shouting at once.

"Where's Ms. Dalton?"

"Yeah, she's always on time."

"Here she comes."

"I can't stand the suspense."

"Who has the hat?"

"Get Tommy's — he has the biggest head. It will hold a million pieces of paper."

Irene Dalton stood next to her desk, looking around the classroom. She smiled a huge grin. "Everyone ready?" It was easy to see that she was as excited as the class.

"Ready!" Lucy yelled.

"Me, too." Steve said.

There was a general shout of agreement that everyone was ready.

"Okay," Ms. Dalton said. "I've got all these little pieces of paper with a name on each. Now watch me throw them into this hat."

The room was totally silent.

"We're ready. Who wants to draw first?"

The room stayed silent. Then there was a general shuffling of feet and clearing of throats. No one seemed to want to go first.

"What's wrong?" Ms. Dalton asked. "Cold feet? Want to call the whole thing off?"

"Of course not," Jason said. "I'll go first. Whoever gets me will be a lucky person."

Jason strolled to the front of the room, taking his time.

"Move it, Jason," Andy yelled.

Jason put his hand into the hat and vigorously mixed up the pieces of paper. He gazed out over the heads of the students in the class and kept shuffling the papers.

"Jason," Nora yelled. "What are you doing? Pull out a piece of paper."

Closing his eyes, Jason pulled.

"Give me the paper," Ms. Dalton said.

Jason handed her the paper. She opened it and read, "Jason will go to Mitch Pauley's home."

Mitch clapped his hand to his forehead. "My poor parents."

"Okay," Ms. Dalton said. "I'll write a list on the blackboard of who is going where." She turned and wrote.

"Who is next?" She asked as she turned back to the class.

"Me," Nora said. She ran up to the hat and pulled out a paper and handed it to Ms. Dalton.

"Nora is going to Lucy Armanson's."

Jen, seeing that Nora had been eager, decided to follow Nora's lead. She went up to the hat and drew.

"Jen goes to Denise Hendrix's house."

"*I* wanted to go there," Mitch said.

"I told you, *Denise* wouldn't be there, dummy," Tommy said.

"Oh, yeah?" Mitch said.

Jen was startled to realize that her first thought when she heard she was going to be at Denise's house was that she would be where Tony was. She couldn't believe she could feel like that. She stole a look at Steve out of the corner of her eye. He wasn't even looking at her. But she still felt strange. If she loved Steve, how could she still be interested in Tony?

They continued the drawing.

Denise pulled the red and purple scarf she was wearing around her neck a little tighter. "Well, if I no longer have a home, I guess I'd better find another one."

She pulled a paper out of the hat and handed it to Ms. Dalton.

"Well, Denise," Ms. Dalton said, "you go to Mia's."

"My mother will be ecstatic," Mia said. "Someone with real hair."

"Okay, Mia. You next," Denise shouted.

Mia pulled her paper.

"Mia is going to Jen's."

Jen could hardly keep from laughing out loud. She met Nora's glance, and they both looked away quickly. Jen could just picture her father with Mia. Someone was going to have to bend.

Steve walked up to the hat, relieved that he wouldn't be living at Jen's.

"Steve goes to Tommy's," Ms. Dalton cried out.

Lucy ran up to the front of the room, grabbed a piece of paper, and handed it to Ms. Dalton.

"Lucy to Steve's."

"Now me," Tracy called out.

"Go to it, Tracy," Mitch shouted.

"And Tracy goes to Susan's," Irene Dalton said.

They continued until everyone who was part of the experiment had drawn a paper. Jen quickly copied as many of the names off of the blackboard as she had time to do before Ms. Dalton started talking. Jen wrote:

> *Jen to Denise*
> *Jason to Mitch*
> *Denise to Mia*

Steve to Tommy
Lucy to Steve
Mia to Jen
Tracy to Susan
Nora to Lucy

Ms. Dalton yelled over the noise in the classroom, "Okay. Tonight, go home, tell your parents where you are going to be. Tomorrow we will talk about all the arrangements that have to be made for the Switch. The experiment will start on Monday, so you have the weekend to get ready."

The class pushed out of the room, reading the names on the pieces of paper they had clutched in their hands. Some of them looked happy; some looked a little worried; and some looked a little stunned. They went through the day barely hearing what went on in every other class. The rest of the students in Cedar Groves Junior High looked at the eighth grade social studies class with new respect. After all, they were embarking on a big new experience.

At the end of the day, Jen and Nora went back to Jen's house. They collapsed at the table in the kitchen and Jen let out a sigh. "Can you imagine it? I'll be at Denise's. In that gorgeous bedroom with the huge brass bed, and the fluffiest towels I've ever seen in her bathroom."

Jen didn't mention her feeling about

Tony . . . yet. But suddenly she noticed that Nora was very quiet. Much too quiet for Nora.

"Hey," Jen said softly. "What's up? You are very quiet."

"Nothing is up," Nora said with annoyance. She got up from the table and walked over to the big Morris-the-Cat cookie jar on the blue counter. She pulled out a huge chocolate cookie and frowned. "Honestly, Jen, don't you ever have anything healthy in this house?"

"Come off it, Nora. You know Jeff cares about healthy food and all that stuff. What you are holding is probably made with all the best ingredients. What is with you?"

Nora took a bite of the cookie and chewed it with great concentration. Then she threw it on the counter and turned to Jen. Her big brown eyes were troubled. "You're going to hate me."

Jen laughed with amazement. "Nora, how could I ever hate you? That's just nutsy."

"You'll see," Nora said firmly. "You'll see."

"Nora, will you spit out what is bothering you and stop all these strange 'you'll see's!'"

Nora turned away so that Jen couldn't see her face. "I'm nervous about going to Lucy's."

"And you made fun of me," Jen said, and shook her head.

Nora whirled around and faced Jen. "See? I told you you'd hate me."

"Oh, Nora, stop the hate stuff. But I just don't understand what you're nervous about. I mean, we've had parties at Lucy's. We've had sleepovers there. We've camped out in her backyard. What are you afraid of?"

"I'm not afraid, Jen. I'm just nervous. The last time Lucy had a party, I went on and on to Dr. Armanson about how I was going to be a doctor and all that kind of thing. I know he thought I was arrogant and dumb, just assuming anyone could be a doctor. He probably won't even speak to me."

Jen couldn't believe that Nora was really concerned. "You'll have a wonderful time. You can talk doctor stuff with him."

Nora snorted. "Jen, now *you're* nuts. I don't really know any doctor stuff. I just pretend."

"You know, Nora. You do."

Jen twisted a strand of long dark hair around her finger and gazed at the floor. She took the cookie Nora had thrown on the counter and began to eat it. "Anyway," she said, "I'm the one with something to be nervous about."

"You?" Nora shouted. "You will be living like a princess. You'll have silk sheets and caviar for breakfast and more fluffy towels than you could use in a lifetime."

"That's not what I'm talking about," Jen said seriously.

"Well, what are you talking about?" Nora asked. "Now *you* are being mysterious."

"I'm talking about living in the same house as Tony," Jen said, so softly that Nora could hardly hear her.

"I think you said something about Tony," Nora said. "You spoke so low I could hardly hear you. What about Tony? I thought you liked Steve."

"I thought I did, too," Jen said. "But when I found out I was staying at Denise's, the first thing I thought about was Tony. I mean, being with him all the time. Do you think there is something wrong with me? I must be a terrible girl."

"I don't think there's anything terrible about you. But we could ask Sally. She knows a lot more about this boy-girl stuff than we do."

"You went out with Brad," Jen said.

"I had two dates with him. That doesn't make me Ann Landers."

Jeff Crawford came through the back door just then and walked into the kitchen.

"Who needs Ann Landers?" he asked. "And would Andy Landers do just as well?"

Jen wondered whether she should talk to Jeff about Steve, but then decided no matter how much she liked him, he was still a grown-up and you didn't discuss your love life with grown-ups . . . except maybe a grandmother.

Chapter 6

At seven o'clock that evening, in a yellow house four blocks away, Lucy Armanson sat at the dinner table with her mother and father and pushed the food on her plate around. When she wasn't pushing the food around, she was pushing up the sleeves of her bulky white sweater or adjusting the wide belt around her narrow hips.

"Lucy," her mother said, "you aren't eating."

"Not hungry," Lucy mumbled.

Dr. Armanson looked up from the steak he was cutting and gave Lucy a quick, professional once-over. He reached over and put the back of his hand on Lucy's forehead.

"Very professional," Lucy said. "When mother does that, you tell her no one can tell a person's temperature that way."

"But I'm a doctor," Lucy's father said. "I have special abilities."

"Oh, Dad. Come on."

"Okay, Lucy, so you don't have a fever. What do you have?" Mrs. Armanson asked.

"I'm fine," Lucy said. "I'm just not hungry. Isn't that allowed?"

Dr. Armanson shook his head. "I have never seen you push steak around on your plate. It's usually in your stomach before your mother and I have had a chance to cut ours."

Suddenly a thoughtful look crossed Mrs. Armanson's face. She raised her eyebrows and asked, "Didn't you do the switch thing at school today . . . pick out where everyone was going?"

Lucy nodded and vigorously began cutting her steak.

"Where are you bound for?" Dr. Armanson asked.

Lucy put down her work. "I'm bound for Steve Crowley's house."

"You'll get good food there. That's for sure. Joe Crowley's restaurant is the best in town."

"That's just it. He'll be in the restaurant all the time, and I'll be alone with his mother. And she's supposedly the most intellectual woman in Cedar Groves."

"Thanks a lot, Lucy," Mrs. Armanson said.

"I don't mean that the way it sounds," Lucy said. "I mean she is always studying strange subjects, like Egyptian flowers, and medieval history, and Spanish literature. She takes every course the university gives, practically. What am I going to talk to her about?"

"Lucy, I thought Steve was your friend," Dr. Armanson said.

"Well, he is," Lucy answered.

"You've been to parties at his house and barbecues in the summer. Right?"

"Yes, Dad, but what is your point?"

"Well, you must have met his mother before. What did you talk to her about then?"

Lucy pushed her chair back and got up from the table. "That's not like being alone with her for a week, and having to make conversation," Lucy said.

"Lucy," Mrs. Armanson said, "which child is coming here? You haven't told us yet."

"Nora is coming here. Nora Ryan."

"Well, now, you don't suppose she's worried about what she is going to talk to us about, do you?" Mrs. Armanson asked.

Lucy shrugged. "I guess not. Nora is always so sure of herself."

"I thought you were sure of yourself," Dr. Armanson said to Lucy.

"Dad, not as sure as I thought I was."

The weekend seemed endless to the eighth grade class. More phone calls were made back and forth between the group than had ever been made in the history of Cedar Groves phone lines. Bags were packed and unpacked hundreds of times. The instructions were read, interpreted, and reinterpreted hundreds of times. And some of the students were ready to withdraw from the whole experiment hundreds of times.

Nora and Jen spent the entire weekend either together or on the phone. They examined each other's duffels carefully and each gave advice to the other that was ignored.

"Jen," Nora said firmly. "You cannot, I repeat, cannot take your flannel pajamas with the ducks on them to Denise's. It isn't even cold enough for flannels."

Jen tightened her mouth. "I don't care what the temperature is. I am taking, I repeat, taking, and wearing, I repeat, wearing, my ducky flannels. They make me feel good, safe, secure."

"Can't you feel secure in those wonderful satin things Tracy gave you last Christmas?"

"No! I always feel like I'm going to slip out of them any minute."

Nora was silent. Then Jen said, "And what about you? You are taking a whole bag of granola bars. I saw them with my very own eyes. And Ms. Dalton said not to take unnecessary things. You should talk.

Ducky pajamas are a lot more important than granola bars."

"I'd rather not starve to death," Nora said. "How do I know what kind of food the Armansons eat? It may be just like the Hendrixes' . . . full of cholesterol."

"Never," Jen said. "He's a doctor. He knows about nutrition and all that stuff. I'd probably starve there, not you. I'll bet there isn't a Twinkie in the house."

"Promise?" Nora said. Then she smiled and the girls grabbed each other in a warm hug. "Everything is going to be wonderful for everyone. I know it."

"Promise?" Jen said, not sounding sure.

And then it was Monday morning. A special school bus came to each eighth-grader's house and picked up the packed bag and delivered it to the house the student was going to. Jen watched the driver take her bag, and her eyes filled with tears. What am I doing? she thought. Who needs this? But when she saw her father waiting at the door to kiss her good-bye, she quickly brushed at her eyes and smiled brightly.

"Talk to you tomorrow," Jen said. She kissed her father, waved to Jeff, and ran down the street.

Once she got away from the house, she felt better. She looked down at her new jeans and shrugged happily in the soft angora sweather she had put on. The over-sized man's jacket she was wearing made her feel really trendy. She was ready for Denise Hendrix's house.

The entire eighth grade social studies class had done what Jen had done, dressed in the clothes that made them feel good. They were as ready to meet their new parents as they would ever be.

At the end of the day, Jen and Nora hugged each other. "Look," Nora said, pointing to a shiny light blue convertible waiting in front of the school.

Barbara Hendrix was at the wheel, waving wildly at Jen. Jen hesitated, but Nora gave her a shove and Jen ran down the steps to the car. As Jen got into the most expensive car she'd ever been in, Mrs. Hendrix said, "I thought I'd just pick you up today . . . to welcome you. But just today. After this you're on your own." Denise's mother smiled and patted Jen's cheek.

Dinner that night was a blur for Jen. A blur of shining silver and delicate crystal, of a maid serving food, of everyone trying to include Jen in the conversation and just making her feel more uptight. And, of course, there was Tony. His dark eyes sparkled in the candlelight, and every now and then he would smile reassuringly at Jen.

After dinner, Barbara Hendrix said, "What would you like to do now, Jen? There's everything in the den: TV, stereo, books. Or do you have homework?"

Jen shook her head. "Everyone was really nice today. They knew we were going to be in our new homes for the first night, so no one gave us any homework. I wish they'd do that more often. But . . . if you don't mind, I'd just as soon go up to my room, read, watch TV there. I know Denise has a set in her room. I'm kind of tired."

Mrs. Hendrix smiled. "Of course, Jen. Do just what you want. Tony, walk Jen upstairs and make sure she knows where all the lights are and that kind of thing."

Jen went up the stairs slowly, aware of Tony next to her. Why did she have to send him with me? Jen thought. He had looked so wonderful in the candlelight. But then so would Steve, Jen thought, trying to be loyal . . . and not feel like a fickle child.

Tony stepped into his sister's room and walked around it, turning on lamps. "The TV is over there. Stereo is on that shelf, and the bathroom is behind that mirrored door. Yell if you need anything." Tony smiled at Jen and her heart flipped. "Glad you were the one who came here, Jen. We could have gotten Jason."

Jen blushed and watched Tony as he walked away. In Denise's room, or what was *her* room for a week, Jen sat down on the bed and just looked around. She had been in this room often, but knowing it was all hers for a week made her feel different. She leaned back against the mound of flowered pillows on the bed, put her hands behind her head, and sighed deeply. Not bad, she thought. She walked into the bathroom and, even though she had showered that morning, she couldn't resist filling the huge tub with hot water, and dumping in a large amount of bubble bath from a crystal bottle on a shelf. She luxuriated in the sea of bubbles and then dried herself on a huge pink towel.

She hesitated as she took her flannel pajamas out of the duffel bag. Nora had been right. They didn't fit into this room. But once she had them on, Jen was glad she had brought them. She got into bed and turned on the TV with the remote control. She could hear voices from downstairs, but she suddenly felt very alone. She thought about her own house with Eric being a pest, and Jeff cleaning up in the kitchen, and her father reading the paper.

Baby, she thought. Are you going to

spend your whole life at home, never having an adventure?

There was a knock at the door and Jen called out, "Come in."

Barbara Hendrix came in and walked over to the bed. She sat down, and Jen smelled her perfume. It was like nothing Jen had ever smelled before, as if it had been made just for Barbara Hendrix.

"Do you have everything you need?" Mrs. Hendrix asked.

"Yes, thank you. Everything. I took a bath with half a tub of bubble bath."

"Good." Barbara Hendrix reached out and touched Jen's pajamas. "I had flannels with ducks when I was about thirteen, too. I loved them. They always made me feel safe."

Jen was amazed. This beautiful, sophisticated woman had once worn ducky pajamas! "That's just the way I feel in them."

Denise's mother laughed. "Not exactly what Denise would wear. Right?"

Jen and Mrs. Hendrix exchanged a look, and they both burst out laughing. "Not unless she could have satin pajamas with some strange and wonderful animal on them," Jen said.

Mrs. Hendrix pushed Jen's hair off her forehead. "Don't feel shy here, Jennie. If you need anything during the night, my bedroom is just two doors away."

Barbara Hendrix leaned over and kissed Jen's cheek. Jennie. From far away, came a voice. Jennie. Her mother must have called her Jennie. Once again, Jen smelled the perfume and again from way back came the memory of another woman sitting on her bed, smoothing her hair, kissing her cheek. It had been a long time.

Jen put her arms around Mrs. Hendrix's neck and hugged her. "I'm going to be fine now. Thank you. I think I'll go right to sleep."

Chapter 7

When the Armansons sat down to dinner, Dr. Armanson sank into his chair at one end of the table and gazed at his wife at the other end. "Everyone in Cedar Groves had either a backache, a stomachache, or a headache today."

"Tired, Harvey?" Elizabeth Armanson asked.

"Exhausted! How was your day?"

Mrs. Armanson looked a little concerned. "It was okay, but I will tell you there are easier things to do than running a day-care center . . . and quieter. All I want is beautiful, wonderful quiet."

Nora thought to herself that she would have to remember to keep her radio down low and the TV in Lucy's room, too. Elizabeth Armanson turned to Nora.

"What are you interested in, Nora? Besides school and boys and clothes . . . all the things Lucy is totally involved in."

Nora cleared her throat. "Well, I would like to be a doctor someday. If I can."

Dr. Armanson peered at Nora. His eyes were sharp under his bushy eyebrows. "You can't just say 'I would like' when it comes to being a doctor. You have to want to be one more than anything else in this world. That's how hard the grind is to get there."

Nora's heart sank. She'd been right. Dr. Armanson thought she was a frivolous kid. Maybe she was. This was going to be some week!

Meanwhile, Lucy was unpacking her clothes and hanging them in Steve's closet. She heard Mrs. Crowley moving around downstairs, and she mentally made a list of all the things she could talk to her about. They had been studying the problems in the Far East in school. She could talk to her about that. Lucy sighed. *That* would be fascinating.

Lucy looked around Steve's room . . . at the football posters on the walls . . . the week's menus in Mr. Crowley's restaurant propped up on his desk . . . the attractive but dark bedspread on the bed: brown and black and beige. Lucy suddenly yearned for her yellow and white bedroom. She was just about to think maybe she'd made a mistake when she heard a sound in the doorway. Carol Crowley was standing there, smiling.

"I thought it might be fun for you to eat at the restaurant tonight. It's busy and lively and. . . ."

"Sure," Lucy said quickly. "Fine."

Mrs. Crowley touched a pink sweater that Lucy had thrown on the bed. "Pretty."

"Thanks," Lucy said. "It's my favorite." Lucy reached for her bag, which was hanging over a chair. "I'm ready, if you are."

"It looks like it might rain. Do you think you need a raincoat?"

Lucy looked out of the window at the clear sky. "I don't think so," she said hesitantly.

"Oh," Mrs. Crowley said. "Maybe you should take it, just in case."

Lucy went to her closet and took out the coat, rather than argue. What was with this lady?

Denise was trying to fit all the clothes she had brought with her into Mia's small closet and bureau. She slammed the closet door shut, hoping everything wouldn't pop out. Then she went into the bathroom Mia shared with the rest of her family. It was a good thing Mia's father was away on business that week. Denise looked about to see where she could put all her cosmetics. There was only one empty shelf in the medicine cabinet. Hardly enough room for her hair stuff, much less anything else. She should have listened to Ms. Dalton and not brought so much, but everything was absolutely essential. Absolutely. There were clean towels on a rack, but only a few, not the piles that were in her own bathroom at home.

This was going to be a strange week.

Mitch's older brother Mike looked at Jason's skateboard and laughed. "What is that?"

Since Jason was going to be sharing a room with Mike, he thought he'd better be polite and not say what he felt like saying. Something like, What do you *think* it is, you nerd?

Instead he said, as calmly as he could, "It's a skateboard."

Mike laughed again. "Don't you think you're too old for that? You should be into other, more mature, things."

Suddenly Jason was interested. After all, inside he was a very mature person. It just didn't show much. Yet. "Mature, like what?" Jason asked.

Mike was as much of a jock as Mitch. In fact, it was Mike that Mitch was always trying to copy. "Well," Mike said with assurance, "you should be into some sport.

Basketball, football, track. Something like that."

Jason thought of his recent karate failure and swallowed hard. "You think I could do it?" he asked.

"Of course you can. You'll impress the girls, too. A skateboard is for kids, Jas."

Girls, Jason thought, and Moni came to mind. Well, it didn't have to be an older woman like Moni. He could start on someone a little less frightening.

Wow. What a week this was going to be!

Tommy's parents and Steve sat around a big maple table in the kitchen and ate dinner. Steve thought of the restaurant and wondered what was going on there. Were they busy? Did his father need him? But he pushed those thoughts out of his mind when Mrs. Ryder began asking him questions about school and what he liked to do. She made all the small talk parents make to try to put kids at ease. She didn't really know she was only making him more nervous.

She turned to her husband and said, "Isn't it nice, Bob, not to have the entire dinner table conversation taken up with girls, girls, girls?"

"Nothing wrong with talk about girls, Madge. It's healthy for a growing boy. Do you have a girlfriend, Steve?"

Steve thought about Jen. Was she his girlfriend?

"Well," Steve said, reddening. "I'm not sure."

"Do you have one you'd *like* to be your girlfriend?"

"Bob," Mrs. Ryder said. "Leave him alone. You're embarrassing him."

"What's to embarrass?" Mr. Ryder asked. "He either has a girl he likes or he doesn't. If he does, I'll teach him everything I taught Tommy . . . about how to interest a girl, impress her. That kind of thing. It can't hurt for a guy to learn that early."

Steve thought about Tommy. He certainly had confidence . . . and girls *did* like him. Didn't they? Maybe it would be good to take a few lessons from Mr. Ryder.

What a week this was going to be!

Tracy and the Hillards sat in the den, eating on TV tables so Mr. Hillard could watch the football game on TV.

Tracy was determined to watch every move Mrs. Hillard made, everything she said. Tracy was sure that Susan had gotten her ability to be so assertive, so sure of herself, and so able not to care about what people thought about her from her mother. Tracy didn't want to be like Susan, but she wished she had a little of Susan's "I'm right" quality. So Mrs. Hillard was going to be her role model.

"Sure you don't mind?" Mr. Hillard asked his wife, shaking his head in the direction of the TV set.

"It's fine. Just fine," she answered.

Football was not one of Tracy's favorite things in life, but she guessed Mrs. Hillard must love it. But as she watched Susan's mother she noticed that she never looked at the set, but just talked softly to Tracy all through dinner. When she wasn't fussing over Mr. Hillard, she was fussing over Tracy.

Tracy waited for a sign that Mrs. Hillard was like Susan, but not a mean word came out of her mouth all evening long. Tracy decided that Mrs. Hillard was just being on her best behavior because it was Tracy's first night. Soon her real personality would come through.

What a strange week this was going to be.

Mia sat at the table in the kitchen watching Jeff fix dinner. Ted Mann wasn't home yet, and Eric was just staring at Mia's hair. Mia reached out to put a finger topped by a green fingernail into the bowl that Jeff was mixing mashed potatoes in. He slapped her hand.

"Never," he said. "Never will a green fingernail go into any food I'm preparing."

Eric kept staring at Mia. "Is that really the color of your hair? I mean is it really purple with orange streaks?"

"Today it is," Mia answered solemnly. "Tomorrow, who knows?"

Ted Mann came into the house, slammed the door after him, and came into the kitchen. He stopped short when he saw Mia, but then managed to say cheerfully, "Well, Mia. Glad to have you."

Jeff stopped mashing the poatoes and looked at Mia from top to bottom. "You know, Jen has a lot of clothes in her closet. You might want to try wearing some of them."

Mia looked down at the black top with silver stars on it and the red skirt over lavender tights. Uh-oh, she thought, I know what's coming. He is going to try to change my style.

What a week this will be.

In the morning, Jen's alarm woke her with a start. For a moment she couldn't figure out where she was. The fluffy, plum-colored comforter that covered her was totally unfamiliar. Then she remembered, and she stretched luxuriously. In the bathroom, she couldn't wait to try out the shower. The needles of hot water were just the right strength, and as Jen wrapped herself in a huge bath towel she sighed with delight. There were three hair dryers on a shelf, two curling irons, and one standing hair dryer next to a dressing table. Jen quickly dried her long, dark hair, dressed in jeans and a bright blue sweater, and started to go downstairs.

Then she ran back to the room and carefully put on some eye shadow, blusher, and lip gloss. Tony would probably be at breakfast, wouldn't he? The picture of Steve handing her one long red rose suddenly popped into her head, and she could hardly bear how guilty she felt. But after all, she was only going to be at the Hendrixes' for a week. How much guilt should she feel for one week?

Everyone was already at the breakfast table when Jen came down. Mrs. Hendrix had on a long, red velvet robe and her hair was pulled back with a red ribbon. She looked like the most beautiful woman Jen had ever seen. Mr. Hendrix was reading the morning paper, and Tony was sipping a glass of orange juice.

"Sleep well?" Barbara Hendrix asked.

"Fine," Jen answered. She turned to Tony and asked him, "Sleep well, Tony?"

Tony looked at Jen through sleepy eyes

and grunted. What he grunted Jen couldn't really tell. And just then a maid came in and stopped next to Jen. "What would you like for breakfast, Miss Jennifer?"

Jen just stared. *Miss* Jennifer. She was beside herself with joy. "Like?" Jen repeated.

"Yes," the maid said. "Eggs? Pancakes? Waffles? French toast?"

"Really?" Jen said.

The maid laughed. "Really."

"I guess pancakes," Jen said. "And bacon if I could."

Mr. Hendrix looked up and smiled. "I like a girl with a good appetite. Denise eats like a bird."

"But Denise has a perfect figure," Jen said.

"Nothing wrong with your figure, Jen," Mrs. Hendrix said. "It's just as good as Denise's."

Jen glowed. She looked at Tony out of the corner of her eyes, but he seemed to be in another world. As if he weren't even at the table. She tried again. "What are *you* having for breakfast, Tony?"

Again Tony just stared at her. "Don't eat breakfast," he replied.

He's almost rude, Jen thought.

Barbara Hendrix saw the strange expression on Jen's face and said quickly,

"Tony, as you can see, is not a morning person. In fact, he is barely civil in the morning. Don't let it bother you."

On the way to school, Jen thought about that. He *was* rude. Steve would never be like that, even in the morning. But then, Jen thought, that really is very mature of Tony not to like the mornings. I mean, what is so great about falling out of bed and having to get ready for school? And sometimes it's raining or snowing or something. It's just because Steve is younger that he is always so good-natured. That can really get boring. But Tony has hidden depths to him.

At lunchtime, the eighth-graders involved in the Great Eighth Grade Switch couldn't wait to get together and go over their night in their new homes. Since there wasn't enough room at one table, they split up and, without thinking much about it, the boys crowded around one table and the girls around another.

"Well," Jen said. "How did it go?"

Lucy shook her head and looked puzzled. "I'm not sure. I think Mrs. Crowley might be a little strange. She insisted that I wear my raincoat when we went out to dinner, and so I did. I mean, I didn't want to argue the first night I was there."

"But it wasn't raining," Jen said.

Lucy shrugged. "I know it. That's what I mean that she might be a little strange."

"Weird," Mia said. "But Jen, I think Jeff is going to try to change my style."

Jen and Nora exchanged a look. "Jeff wouldn't do that," Nora said, "He's so accepting."

"Of course, he wouldn't do that," Jen said tightly. "If you think that about Jeff, you don't know him."

"Well, I may not know him, but I do know when someone wants to change the way I dress. I'm an expert at knowing that," Mia said, turning away from Jen.

"Well," Jen said, smiling. "*I* had a wonderful night." She looked at Denise and said, "Your bath towels alone make the visit worthwhile."

Jen looked away from the table then. She couldn't tell anyone, well, maybe Nora later, about how happy she had felt with Denise's mother. And she certainly couldn't tell anyone about how excitingly withdrawn Tony could be. Almost like a hero in a novel.

"How did it go for you, Nora?" Jen asked, not liking the way Nora hadn't immediately leaped into the discussion, telling everyone exactly what had gone on at the Armanson's.

"I don't think your father likes me, Lucy. I think he thinks I'm a jerk." Nora's voice cracked slightly as she spoke.

"That's ridiculous, Nora," Lucy said firmly. "My father hardly knows you. How could he dislike you?" Lucy sounded irritated, as if Nora had attacked her father.

"Your mother is real nice, Mia," Denise said, smoothing down the long blonde hair that was hanging over one shoulder. "But this morning, she had me make my bed. I mean, *make my bed*."

Mia's eyes narrowed. "Well, everyone makes his or her own bed every morning. You are just too overprivileged."

This is not going the way I thought it would, Jen thought. Everyone is so defensive. But then Tracy said in her low, drawling voice, "Well, I'll tell you one thing . . . Susan did not get to be Susan by watching her mother. Her mother is a very sweet, nice woman."

"Is Susan like her father?" Nora asked. Tracy suddenly became silent. "I'm not supposed to talk about my foster parents. Remember? Ms. Dalton said so."

"Tracy, that's not 'talking' about them," Denise said with an edge in her voice.

"Talking is talking," Tracy said primly. "And I'm not." She tightened her lips and looked noble.

At the boys' table, Jason and Steve were deep in conversation. "Mitch's brother said I should get into some sport. What do you think, Steve?"

Steve hesitated. "Remember the karate business, Jason?"

"Well, just because I wasn't great at karate, doesn't mean I couldn't turn out to be a whiz at something else."

Steve was silent. Then he said, "Tommy's father wants to give me some pointers on attracting girls. Tommy sure does all right."

Jason shook his head. "I've had enough of girls for a while. But you could take notes and tell me whatever Mr. Ryder tells you."

Steve looked at Jason . . . his bright red hair which, as usual, was sticking up; his skinny body; and the skateboard resting next to him on the floor. I don't think my notes will help him much, Steve thought.

Chapter 8

After school, the Great Eighth Grade Switch group gathered on the steps of the junior high. They awkwardly milled around, not knowing exactly where to go.

"What should we do?" Lucy asked. "I don't feel right about asking you to the Crowleys' house. I mean, maybe Mrs. Crowley doesn't like a bunch of kids in her house."

"She wouldn't mind at all," Steve said. "At least she doesn't when I bring kids home. But . . . I have to get home . . . I mean, to my . . . foster home. . . . I have things to do. Important things."

Steve didn't want to miss seeing Mr. Ryder the minute he came home. There was a lot Mr. Ryder could teach him and he was ready.

"What important things?" Jen asked.

"Just things," Steve said vaguely.

"Well, I'm not sure I should ask every-one to Denise's house . . . I mean, my house, either. Tony might not like it."

"TONY?" everyone yelled at once.

"What's Tony got to do with anything?" Denise asked.

Jen pushed her long hair off of her face, and pulled her bright red jacket tighter around her body. "Well, he does live there, too, you know. I should get home, too. I have a lot of homework."

"We hardly have any homework," Tracy said. She looked at Jen with big, puzzled blue eyes.

"Oh, Tracy, don't be so . . . so . . . Tracy."

"What does that mean?" Nora asked.

"I have to go home," Jen said, ignoring Nora. Tony will be home soon, she thought, and maybe we can have a little time to-gether before dinner.

"I guess you could all come to my house . . . or Mia's house . . . or whoever's house it is. I'm confused," Denise said.

"Sure you could," Mia said. "My mother is at work, and she won't mind."

Denise bent down to lace up the high boots she was wearing. They looked like they had come out of the nineteenth cen-tury, and the other girls looked at them with envy. "Wait a minute," she said. "I forgot. I promised Mrs. Stevens I'd start dinner tonight. I think I'd better get home and read all her instructions."

Nora put her hand over her mouth to keep from bursting out laughing. "*You* are going to cook dinner?"

"Glad I'm not eating there," Jason said.

"Yes, I am, too," Denise said frostily. "What is so funny about my making dinner? Any jerk can fix dinner."

"Wanna bet?" Jason said, and rolled away on his skateboard. Mike was going to come home right after school and show Jason how to shoot some baskets. Jason practiced deep breathing, trying to get ready for Mike, hoping to show him how much of a jock Jason Anthony could be.

When Jason got to the Pauleys' house, as he really thought of it, Mike was in the kitchen, drinking a tall glass of something beige-colored. "Want some?" he asked Jason.

The color of the drink was upsetting to Jason, so he asked nervously, "What is it?"

"It's an energy builder," Mike said. "You, of all people, should drink this."

Jason watched Mike pour a huge glass of the stuff, and Jason took it gingerly. "Drink it," Mike ordered.

Jason forced himself to drink it as quickly as he could, but nothing could take away the taste of fresh yeast and who knew what else. Mike watched Jason carefully. "Good, isn't it?"

Jason nodded his head, trying to catch his breath.

"Okay, now everyone outside for basket practice."

They practiced for an hour. Jason tried, but the ball seemed to land on his head more than near the basket. He ran after the ball; he held it in the position Mike demonstrated; he threw it with all his strength; but not once did the ball go into the basket. It didn't even skim the hoop. After sixty minutes of this, Mike looked at Jason's red face, the sweat running down his cheeks, and his disappointed look, and said, "You're doing fine. You just need a little more practice. Tomorrow, same time, same place."

Jason went upstairs to Mike's room. The room was filled with trophies and ribbons and framed pictures of Mike with his teams. Jason threw himself on the bed and stared at the ceiling. What was wrong with him? Why couldn't he measure up in some way? Either in sports or with girls or in his classes. Why was he always the clown? Then he heard Mike saying, "You just need a little more practice." Mike was right. All he had to do was try a little harder. He smiled and got up, stood on his skateboard, and rolled around the room.

From downstairs came Mike's voice. "Cut it out, Anthony."

Jen walked into the Hendrix house and heard nothing . . . not one sound. Then, Mimi, the maid who had served breakfast, came to the hallway. "Hello, Miss Jennifer. Would you like something to eat? Denise always has tea and cookies after school."

"How come, Mimi," Jen asked, "you call me 'Miss' Jennifer and you call Denise, 'Denise'?"

"You're a guest, Miss. Denise lives here."

"But I'm not supposed to be a guest, I'm supposed to be one of the family, so just call me Jennifer. Okay?"

"Okay." Mimi smiled and noticed Jennifer trying to look into the rooms that ran off the hallway. "Tony is in the den, studying."

Jen blushed and nodded. She walked into the den and stood there silently. The sun was coming through the window and fell on Tony's dark hair, making it shine. He looked up and smiled at Jen. "Hi. Come on in. You're home early. No good deeds to do today?"

Jen smiled, too. "You mean like whales

and senior citizens and animals? Well, no. None today."

"If you have any studying to do, why not bring your books in here and join me?"

"Thanks. I have oodles," she lied. "I'll run and get my books." She raced into the hall and picked up a stack of books she had thrown on a bench. Her heart beat rapidly as she pictured the intimacy of studying quietly wih Tony. Suddenly Steve's face came into her mind. Never mind Steve. Hadn't he said he had important things to do? Like what?

She went back into the den and sank into a large velvet chair. Tony raised his head from the history book he was reading and smiled. Then he went back to his studying . . . and that was that. He never said another word, just studied, and made notes.

Jen tried to read a novel for English, but all she was aware of was Tony's even breathing. How mature of him to study so conscientiously. To not be distracted by anything. But then again maybe there was nothing about her that *was* distracting. But if Steve was in the same room with her, she couldn't imagine him so grown-up and just studying.

Suddenly she leaped out of the chair. "My father," she shouted.

"What's wrong with him?" Tony asked.

"I have to call him . . . every day. He'll have the police out after me if I don't."

Tony smiled and looked at Jen's flushed face and her hazel eyes wide with anxiety. "Call him right now, then. There's a phone on that table." He motioned with his head to a leather-topped table near a window.

Jen would have preferred to be alone when she spoke to her dad, but she didn't know how to tell Tony that. So she just dialed her father's office number. When she had him on the line, she said, "Dad. Everything is just fine. Just great. How are you?"

"Are you sure you're all right, Jen?" her father asked.

"I'm sure, Dad."

"Are you getting enough sleep? Eating right? Dressing warmly enough?"

Jen looked at Tony out of the corners of her eyes. How could her father ask such baby questions?

"Dad," she whispered. "I've only been here one night."

"It seems like forever," her father said plaintively.

Jen ignored the tone and asked, "You're being nice to Mia?"

"Of course we're being nice to Mia. Do you think we're monsters? Mia is . . . interesting."

"She thinks Jeff is trying to change her style," Jen said, giggling.

"It wouldn't hurt," her father answered.

"I know what you mean," Jen laughed. "Listen, I've got to go. Talk to you tomorrow."

"Don't forget!"

"I won't forget, Dad."

Chapter 9

When Denise got home to the Stevens' house, she went into the kitchen immediately and read the instructions on a piece of paper stuck to the refrigerator door.

One: Take casserole of lasagna out of freezer.
Two: Set oven at 350 degrees.
Three: Put lasagna in oven.
Four: Take lettuce and other salad ingredients out of crisper in refrigerator and make a small salad.
Five: Set table in kitchen.

Denise smiled. Nothing could be easier. She carefully followed the instructions, and when Dana Stevens came home from work, Denise was sitting in the living room reading *Harper's Bazaar*. She jumped up as Mrs. Stevens came into the room.

"Everything is ready! I did just like you said and everything is under control."

"Great," Mia's mother said. "I'm starving. I'll just run upstairs and wash up and then we can eat."

Denise went back into the kitchen and looked at the table again. When Mrs. Stevens came downstairs she joined Denise and said, "The table looks lovely, Denise. It really does."

Denise had put flowers from the living room into a bowl and set them in the center of the table. Two candles glowed, giving the table a soft light. She had found real linen napkins in a drawer and folded them into a flat shape and centered them on the plates. Denise smiled with pleasure at the sight of the table. Her mother had taught her when she was ten how to set a table that people would like to eat at.

Mrs. Steveins went to the oven and opened it. She took a pot holder and grabbed hold of the casserole. Then she stopped and turned to look at Denise.

"What's wrong?" Denise asked.

Mrs. Stevens bit her lip, not quite smiling. "You forgot to turn it on."

Denise walked over to Dana Stevens and peered into the oven. "Turn what on?"

"The oven, Denise. You didn't turn it on. Nothing cooks unless the oven is *on*."

Denise walked over to a counter and picked up the instructions Mrs. Stevens had left. She read aloud: " 'Set oven at 350 degrees. Put lasagna in oven.' That's *all* it says."

Mrs. Stevens sat down at the table and stared at Denise with disbelief. "But I didn't think I had to tell you to turn the oven on. I mean, how did you think the lasagna was going to defrost?"

Denise sat down, too. "I guess I didn't think. I mean, I don't do this sort of thing usually. Cook, that is."

Now Mrs. Stevens couldn't help herself. She burst out laughing. "This isn't cooking, Denise. This is heating."

Denise pushed her blonde hair off of her forehead and stared at a long, perfectly polished fingernail. "I'm sorry," she murmured.

"It's okay, I'll just turn the oven up real high and this will heat in no time. Don't fret. We'll start with the salad now."

Denise took the salad out of the refrigerator and placed it in front of Mrs. Stevens. It looked beautiful with roses made of radishes around the rim of the bowl. "Mimi, the maid we have, taught me how to do that."

"It's lovely," Mrs. Stevens said. She poured dressing over the salad and started to mix it up. Once again, she stopped. She picked up a piece of lettuce from the bowl and held it up.

"Now what?" Denise asked.

"Denise . . . dear . . . did you wash the lettuce before you made the salad?"

"Wash it?" Denise asked softly.

"Yes. I didn't wash it when I put it in the refrigerator. Didn't you notice all those little black specks in it?"

Denise's shoulders slumped. "I guess not." Her little dangling earrings made of silver and pearl tinkled as she shook her head despairingly.

"Denise," Mrs. Stevens said, suddenly standing up. "How about it if we go out to dinner? Just tonight."

Denise smiled, a beautiful, bright grin. "Wonderful. And it's my treat."

"You're on," Mrs. Stevens said.

"Mrs. Stevens," Denise said. "I'll do better next time. I mean, any jerk can cook a meal."

Dr. Armanson didn't come home for dinner that night. Mrs. Armanson said to Nora, "He's making rounds at the hospital and said he'd be late."

Dinner was better for Nora without him there. She talked easily with Lucy's mother, about her work at the day-care center, about her own mother's legal work, about her feelings about being a doctor.

"Does Dr. Armanson come home this late often?" Nora asked.

"Often," Mrs. Armanson said. "It's part of the territory with being a doctor, Nora. You have to be prepared for that."

"I am . . . really," Nora answered as the front door slammed and Harvey Armanson came into the den.

"Sorry I missed dinner, sweetie," he said as he kissed his wife's cheek. "Things were rough today, and they are going to be rougher tomorrow."

"How come?" Elizabeth Armanson asked.

"Mary has a terrible cold and I told her not to come in tomorrow. I have a feeling she's going to be sick the rest of the week."

"Mary is Dr. Armanson's receptionist," Mrs. Armanson explained to Nora.

"Call the agency, Harvey. They must have someone they can send. You can't manage without help of some kind."

"Liz, by the time I show some new person from the agency what to do, I could do it myself."

"You're wrong, Harvey . . . and stubborn. Get help!"

It just came to Nora suddenly and before she could change her mind she said,

"I can do it. I can help you . . . be your receptionist after school, I mean."

Dr. Armanson looked at Nora, at the head of brown curls framing her face, at the eagerness in her eyes, and the parted lips. "Nora, it's a hard job. Hard even for an adult. You're dealing with anxious people in the office; impatient people on the phone; sick people, and people who think they're sick."

"I can do it, Dr. Armanson. Really. Let's go to your office right now and just show me what to do."

Dr. Armanson looked at his wife. She shrugged and said, "It can't hurt to try her for a day, Harvey. Nora is bright and eager and she may be just fine. She's better than nothing," Liz Armanson said.

Gee, thanks, Nora thought.

Dr. Armanson stood up and held out a hand to Nora. "Okay. Let's try it. We'll go to the office after dinner and I'll show you where things are. But if I don't feel it's working out, you have to accept my decision. No tears, no begging, no trouble."

Nora could hardly contain her happiness. She was going to work in a real doctor's office!

"Wait a minute," Dr. Armanson said. "What time can you be here tomorrow? You do have school."

"I'll come as soon as I get out. My last

period is study period and I'm sure Mr. Donovan will let me out if I tell him that you need me. I can be here by two."

"That's okay," Harvey Armanson said. "My office hours start at one-thirty tomorrow. I can manage for a half hour. Nora . . . I hope we know what we're doing."

Later, up in her room, Nora gazed at the phone next to her bed. Impulsively, she picked it up and dialed Denise's number. When she heard Jen's voice, she whispered into the phone, "Jen, I'm going to work in Dr. Armanson's office tomorrow after school. Can you believe it?"

"Nora, do you know what to do? I mean, what are you going to do?"

"Nothing hard. Answer the phone, take messages, show people into the doctor's office. That kind of thing. I'm not going to perform surgery, Jen. Don't worry. Listen, I don't want to tie up this phone too long. I'll see you tomorrow." Nora hung up and stretched out in her bed. Dr. Nora Ryan, she said to herself. She heard her receptionist, saying to her in the future, "Dr. Ryan, your office is overflowing with patients. What are we going to do?"

Jen sat on the edge of the bed, hardly able to believe what Nora had told her.

Silently she worried about whether Nora was going to be able to take care of Dr. Armanson's office. A knock at the door interrupted her thoughts. "Come in," she said.

Barbara Hendrix came into the room. She was wearing beige pants and a soft, fuzzy yellow sweater. Again there was the perfume that Mrs. Hendrix wore, filling the room with a light, spicy smell. "I just want to say good-night."

Jen smiled and moved over on the bed so that Denise's mother could sit on the edge. "Are you happy here, Jen?" she asked.

"I am. Really." She paused and added in a low voice, "I like it when you come in here at night. It makes me feel ... well ... nice."

"It makes me feel nice, too, Jen," Mrs. Hendrix said. She leaned over and kissed Jen's cheek and then took Jen into her arms and hugged her. She held Jen for just the right amount of time. Not too long to embarrass Jen and not too short a time to make the hug unsatisfying.

Steve gathered together the garbage from the Ryders' kitchen and carted it out to the big pails in the garage. As he was lifting one large bag of garbage, he heard footsteps behind him. Mr. Ryder helped him hoist the bag into the pail.

"Well, Stevie-boy, have you decided whether you have a girlfriend or not?"

"Yeah. I have . . . decided . . . I guess I do have or I'd like to have."

"Well, want a little advice? I know your father is so busy in the restaurant that maybe he doesn't have time to just shoot the breeze with you."

Sure he does, Steve thought. We talk about peeling potatoes and scrubbing pots and ordering more tomatoes all the time. Steve smiled to himself at the thought of his father telling him how to get a girl. It just wasn't something Joe Crowley would do. And it wasn't something Steve wanted him to do. It was okay from Mr. Ryder, but not from his own father.

Mr. Ryder leaned against the garage wall. "Well, I can only talk about my own experience. You have to remember I was a boy a long time ago, but how much could things have changed since I was your age? Anyway, the best thing to do, back then, was to play hard-to-get. Don't let the girl know you like her."

Steve frowned. How could he do that to Jen? Anyway, she knew he liked her already. "I don't know, Mr. Ryder," Steve said. "Jen and I have known each other a long time . . . since kindergarten. I couldn't pretend with her."

"All the more reason," Mr. Ryder said, "to add a little spice to things. She probably takes you for granted. You have to make her really notice you as an attractive boy. You have to play up to the prettiest girl in your class. Who is that?"

Jen, Steve thought, but what he said was, "Denise, I guess. Denise Hendrix."

"Okay," Mr. Ryder said. "When you get to school tomorrow, and Jen, I gather that is the girl's name, is around at the same time Denise is around, you just talk to Denise, smile at her, you know, just be nice to her . . . and make sure Jen sees you. Understand?"

Steve nodded.

"You have to be debonair," Mr. Ryder said. "You know."

I don't know, Steve thought, but before he left for school the next morning he went to his room and looked up the word debonair in the dictionary. " 'Debonair,' " he read aloud. " 'Of pleasant manners, courteous. Sprightly.' " I think I'm in way over my head, Steve thought, but I might as well try it. Mr. Ryder should know . . . and maybe Jen does take me for granted a little.

After dinner, Tracy helped Mrs. Hillard with the dishes, while Mr. Hillard went into the den to read and watch TV. Her own father always helped clean up after meals, but Mr. Hillard didn't seem to think there was any need for him to help at all.

The phone rang as Mrs. Hillard was putting away the pots, and she picked it up, tucked it under her chin, and kept stacking pots. "Tomorrow?" she said. "I don't know, Kathy. It would be hard to take your time at the hospital. I have three other appointments and I promised to bake a cake for the PTA cake sale and. . . . I know. . . . I understand . . . but. . . . Oh, all right, I'll do it. Don't worry, I'll manage somehow."

She hung up and wrote on her calendar, which was already filled with scribbles. Mr. Hillard called from the den. "Can you bring me something cold to drink, honey?"

Tracy watched Mrs. Hillard put down her pencil and go to the refrigerator. Why didn't Mrs. Hillard tell Mr. Hillard to get his own cold drink? Susan would have, in no uncertain words. Susan would say that even to her father. And Mr. Hillard *was* a little lazy. That was for sure. And Mrs. Hillard was a real puzzle.

The next morning, the eighth grade was gathered on the steps of Cedar Groves Junior High, as usual. Jen was talking to Nora, trying to calm her down, which was nearly impossible, but Jen wasn't really listening. She was watching Steve out of the corner of her eyes. He was strange today, no doubt about that. He had barely said hello to her, and now he was talking to Denise. But talking in such a funny way. He was bouncing around, and when he wasn't bouncing, he was bowing and smiling a big, dumb smile. Jen waved to him when he looked her way, but he didn't even wave back. He just turned back to Denise and bowed again.

"Nora," Jen said. "Steve isn't talking to me this morning."

"What do you mean?" Nora asked. "Of course, he's talking to you. Why wouldn't he talk to you?"

"I don't know. But look, he's over there with Denise."

Nora watched Steve for a few minutes. "Why do you suppose he's jumping around like that?"

"How should I know?" Jen said. "But he certainly is being rude to me and charming to Denise."

"You call that charming?" Nora asked. "I think he might have some odd disease ... that's what is making him so jumpy."

"You *always* think everyone has some odd disease. He's not sick. He is just ignoring me."

Denise, meanwhile, was observing Steve. Finally she said, "Steve, what is *wrong* with you? Why are you jumping around like that?" She took off a wide red ribbon she had around her head and retied it into a big bow.

"Don't you think I'm ... well ... sprightly?" Steve asked.

"Sprightly," Denise said. "What does that mean?"

"I'm not sure," Steve answered, looking at Jen again. There was no doubt he was making an impression on her, because she and Nora were talking and looking over at him.

"I have to go, Steve. I have to ... talk to ... to Lucy." Denise moved away from Steve, watching him bow as she went away.

That's courteous, Steve thought. That's good manners. So why do I feel like such a jerk?

Steve smiled at Jen, but for some reason she didn't return the smile. She just turned away.

So, Jen thought, Denise walks away from him and then he smiles at me. Up until then he ignores me. Well, who needs that?

Denise and Lucy sat on the steps of the junior high and compared notes. "I was a total disaster last night," Denise said. "I completely messed up dinner and I felt like a dope."

"That's okay, at least you know what is expected of you. I still can't figure Mrs.

Crowley out. Last night, I mentioned that I was going to do some homework with you after school and she almost freaked out. Kept asking me what time I'd be home and where I was working with you, and even said I should call her and she'd pick me up and drive me back to her house. Now what do you make of that?"

Denise shook her head. "Are you sure you aren't imagining all that?"

"Denise," Lucy said firmly, picking a piece of lint off her sleek green pants, "do I imagine things like that? The lady is like a policewoman. I mean, she's sweet and all that, but she's *strange*."

"Oh, well, only a few more days."

"Denise, this is only the second day."

"I wonder what disastrous thing I'll do today," Denise pondered. "Probably set the house on fire, trying to turn on my hair dryer or something."

Chapter 10

Nora had been right. When she told Mr.
Donovan why she wanted to skip study
period at the end of the day, he told her
to go. She ran all the way to the Armansons' house. Raced upstairs, scrubbed her
hands for five minutes with soap, changed
into a skirt and blouse, and went to Dr.
Armanson's office.

The waiting room was filled with people, but when Harvey Armanson saw Nora,
he beckoned to her to come into his office.
He looked at her hands, which were bright
red and said, "Oh, no. You're not getting
some kind of rash are you?"

Nora looked down at her hands and
then back to Dr. Armanson. "No. I just
scrubbed up real good before I came here.
No germs on my hands."

Dr. Armanson covered a smile with one
hand. "Nora, you aren't going to do open
heart surgery, just answer the phone."

"Yes, Dr. Armanson," she mumbled.

"Okay," he said. "Just do exactly what we went over last night. Ready?"

"Ready," Nora repeated, feeling her stomach move up from where it should normally be. Am I, she thought, ready?

When she took a seat at the receptionist's desk, she smiled at the patients in the office, trying to look reassuring.

"Where's Mary?" a little boy asked with a whine. "I want Mary."

"Yeah," a young woman said, "where's Mary?"

Nora cleared her throat and smiled again. "Mary has a cold and I'll be helping Dr. Armanson until she comes back." She tried to look efficient as she arranged papers that didn't need arranging on the desk.

"I want Mary," the little boy whined again.

Oh, shut up, Nora thought. Don't make trouble.

"You look very young to be doing this kind of work," an aging man said.

"I'm really a lot older than I look," Nora said briskly. "Now would anyone like a magazine or something?"

"The magazines are all out on the tables," the little boy said. "Who needs you to give us one? And I don't like any of the magazines you have anyway."

And I don't like you, Nora thought. Just then the phone rang and she picked it up. After that the afternoon sped by. The phone rang, new patients came in, Dr. Armanson asked for records, and Nora did it all.

When his office hours were over, and Dr. Armanson was leaving to make his rounds at the hospital, he stopped at Nora's desk and looked at her appraisingly. "You're good," he said. "Really good. Thanks for helping me. I'll see you at home. You can leave now. Just turn on the answering machine."

"You mean it?" Nora asked. "You're not just being polite?"

"Do I strike you as the polite type?" Dr. Armanson asked, laughing.

Nora had to laugh, too. "No, I guess you don't."

When he left the office, Nora got up and danced around the room, her arms over her head. "I did it! I did it!"

Tracy went home and watched Mrs. Hillard making Mr. Hillard's favorite dessert — a process that seemed to use up every bowl and pot in the house and took two hours to do.

Jason went home, and Mike had him running around with a football. He didn't mind the running around, but why did Mike have to insist on a half hour of tackling? Mike tackling Jason.

Mia went home and found a navy skirt and frilly blouse laid out on her bed, with little navy pumps on the floor. She went down to the kitchen and said to Jeff, "What's the outfit on my bed for?"

Jeff shrugged. "I just thought you might like it."

"Where did the wild pumps come from? And in my size, too."

"Wild? You call *those* wild?" Jeff shouted. "Look what you have on now."

Mia looked down at her orange suede hightop sneakers with silver laces. "Who would wear those navy things you left in my room? Not me, Jeff. You have to get off my case."

"Never," Jeff mumbled.

When Jen got home, she was sure she and Tony would have time to study together again, just the two of them. But as she walked into the Hendrix house, she heard voices coming from the den. They were all male. Tony had friends. Jen's heart beat faster. She was going to spend some time with Tony's friends!

She walked to the door of the den and

stood there smiling. Tony looked over at her and said, "Hi, Jen."

Jen waited for him to ask her to come in. "Oh," he said to his friends, pointing to Jen, "this is my kid sister's friend Jen. She's part of that crazy eighth grade thing the kids are doing."

The boys all smiled at her and then went back to their conversation. "See you at dinner, Jen," Tony said.

She had been dismissed.

Jen walked up to her room slowly, her cheeks burning. Never, never, would Steve be that unfeeling.

Wrong, Jen thought. Steve is bowing and scraping to Denise. Boys are really the pits. Then she thought, Tony wasn't *really* rude. He was probably just embarrassed when she suddenly appeared. After all, if she had to introduce some boy to all her girlfriends, she would feel awkward.

When Lucy got home Mrs. Crowley was pacing around the living room. "Where were you?" she asked nervously.

Lucy frowned. "I told you I was going to study with Denise. So we were at Mia's house . . . her real house, I mean."

"But I thought you were going to call me and then I would come and get you," Carol Crowley said.

"Mrs. Crowley, Mia lives four blocks from here. I just walked home . . . like I always do."

"In all that traffic?" Mrs. Crowley said.

Lucy stared at Steve's mother. "Traffic? What traffic? There weren't five cars in the streets."

Carol Crowley sighed. "That's a lot."

By the next day, everyone was settling down in their new homes. Things were strange, different, but they all had more of an idea of what to expect.

In the social studies class, Ms. Dalton asked, "Everybody okay? Is it all working out all right? Anybody have anything to say?"

The room was silent.

Jen thought, It *is* wonderful being in the same house with Tony. And he *is* sweet.

Mia thought, Never will I wear those freaky clothes Jeff likes.

Steve thought, I'm really learning a lot from Mr. Ryder. I just don't have the hang of it yet.

Jason thought, I'll find some sport that I really will impress people with.

Tracy thought, Mrs. Hillard is strange.

Lucy thought, Mrs. Crowley is strange.

Denise thought, My fingernails are all broken from all that bed-making and turning on of ovens.

Nora thought, Maybe Dr. Armanson will let me assist him in his examining room today.

Ms. Dalton looked around the room. "So everything is going fine. Right?"

"Right," everyone yelled.

Chapter 11

Thursday morning was rainy and gray and raw. When Jen woke up, she huddled under the plum comforter and listened to the rain beating against the windows. Even the hot shower and the big fluffy towels didn't warm her. To look more cheerful than she felt, she put on a bright red sweater and bright red pants. She pulled her hair back and fastened it with red barettes and then she ran down to breakfast.

Barbara Hendrix smiled when she saw Jen. "You make the world look bright, Jennie dear."

You always make the world look bright, Jen thought. No matter what else good can be said about this week, getting to know Barbara Hendrix makes it all worthwhile. Then Jen looked at Tony, hoping he would notice how she brightened up the room, but he never raised his eyes from the muffin he was buttering.

Mrs. Hendrix saw the look of expectation on Jen's face, and she said, "Jen, dear, how would you like to have a party here Saturday night? It would be a wonderful end to your week. Invite everyone in the experiment and anyone else you'd like, too."

"That's an awful lot of work for you, Mrs. Hendrix," Jen said.

"We'll do it together, and Mimi will help and the rest of the staff, too. I'd like to do it for you."

"I'd love it," Jen said. Tony would come, too, she knew he would. After all, he lived here and it was her last night. It would be wonderful. Maybe I'll even get a new dress, she thought.

She looked over at Tony, about to say something to him, but his total absorption in his cup of coffee made her know this wasn't the right moment. The thought, Maybe there is never a right moment, crept into her mind, but she pushed it away.

At the breakfast table at the Ryders', Mr. Ryder said to Steve, "Well, Stevie-boy, how is it going? Jen getting the message that she's not the only fish in the sea?"

"I'm not sure, Mr. Ryder. I think maybe I'm doing something wrong. Jen isn't looking at me and I think Denise thinks I'm a little bit nuts."

Mr. Ryder wiped his mouth and put down his cup of coffee. "Then, of course, you're doing something wrong. Tell me exactly what you *are* doing."

"I'm being debonair, just like you said," Steve answered.

"Good. Then just keep doing it. It's bound to work."

When Mia got up, she went to the closet and pulled at the doorknob. But it didn't move. She pulled again, but it remained tightly closed. All her clothes were in there; if she couldn't open the door, she had nothing to wear.

She ran down the stairs and raced into the kitchen, where Jeff was making pancakes, and Eric and Mr. Mann were sitting at the table. "Did you do it?" she cried.

"Do what?" Jeff asked, beating the batter in the bowl.

"I know you did," Mia said. "I know it."

Ted Mann held up his hand. "Hold it, Mia, what is this about?"

"Jeff locked up all my clothes," Mia said. "I have nothing to wear to school."

"Of course you do. You can wear that skirt and blouse of Jen's that I put out the other day," Jeff said, putting some pancake batter on the sizzling griddle.

"Never," Mia shouted. "I won't go to school rather than look like a freak."

Mr. Mann stood up and shook his head at Jeff. "If I had done that, you would have had a fit."

He walked over to Mia and patted her shoulder. "You have to go to school every day, Mia. It's part of the whole switch agreement. You know that."

Jeff went over to Mia and tried to push down the spikes of her hair. "Wear the stuff just this once. You'll see, you'll like it. It may change your life."

Mia put her head down on the table. "I'll be the laughingstock of the whole school. I'll look like some preppy jerk."

Eric reached over and pulled at the spikes on Mia's head. "It's real hair," he said.

"Of course it's real hair. What did you think?" Mia asked.

"Who knows?" Eric said.

Lucy was ready to leave the house, when Carol Crowley followed her to the door. "Here," Mrs. Crowley said, handing Lucy a carefully gift-wrapped box.

"What is it?" Lucy asked.

"It's lunch," Mrs. Crowley said proudly.

"Gift-wrapped?" Lucy said with disbelief.

"I thought it would look pretty. It *is* pretty, isn't it?"

Lucy bit her lip. "It's pretty, Mrs. Crowley, but I eat in the cafeteria with all the other kids. We buy our food there. You know that. Steve does it everyday."

Mrs. Crowley tightened the scarf around Lucy's neck and opened the front door. "What I made is more nourishing than that awful cafeteria food. It's better for you."

Lucy left the house and walked to the bus stop, carrying the lunch as if it were a time bomb. On the bus, she sank into a seat next to Denise.

Denise looked at the package and said, "A present for me?"

"It's my lunch," Lucy said with disgust.

"What are you going to do, give it to someone as a birthday present? And what do you mean, it's your lunch? You *buy* your lunch."

"Tell that to Mrs. Crowley," Lucy said.

At lunchtime, the eighth grade switch group found one large table and crowded around it. All eyes were on Lucy's package, which sat in the middle of the table.

"I can't figure out what is with my mother," Steve said. Then he turned to Denise and said, "That package looks almost as lovely as you do."

That's pretty sprightly, he thought.

Denise stared at Steve. "*I* look like a package?" she asked.

"No. No. Of course not," Steve said,

stumbling over his words. "That's not what I meant."

"Then exactly what did you mean?" Denise asked. "No one has ever compared me to a package of lunch before."

Steve looked around the table for help. He met Jen's eyes and saw the cool, hurt expression in them. This wasn't working right at all. Jen wasn't jealous. She wasn't aware of him as a boy other girls would like. She just looked angry and as if she thought he was disgusting.

To get out of being the center of everyone's attention, Steve said, "Open the box, Lucy. Let's see what's in it."

"Whatever it is, it's supposed to be nourishing," Lucy said, dubiously.

Nora's eyes opened wide. "Good. Open it."

Slowly, Lucy undid the satin ribbon, the tape that held the paper closed, and the brightly colored paper. The box was a decorated one that expensive things came in. Lucy opened the box, and then pulled away some tissue paper. First she took out a small thermos of homemade pea soup. Then came a chicken sandwich with crisp green lettuce on it. Then a shiny red apple and then chocolate cookies. Everyone looked at the array of food on the table.

"It *does* look good," Tracy said. "It almost looks good enough to eat."

"Tracy," Jen said, "that's the idea. She's supposed to eat it."

"Oh," Tracy said. "Then why isn't it in a brown paper bag? Like lunch is supposed to be?"

Lucy stood up and pushed the food into the middle of the table. "I'm going to buy some of that brown glop that is on the steam table for my lunch. Anyone want this?"

She left the table and frantic hands grabbed at the food. Nora chewed happily on the chicken sandwich. "She's crazy. She'd rather eat the steam table poison than a wonderful chicken sandwich."

"It's the principle of the thing," Denise said.

"She can have her principles, I'll have the pea soup," Tracy said.

Nora looked around the table and asked, "Listen, I haven't seen Mia all day. Have any of you?"

Tracy stopped drinking her soup and said, "Oh, I forgot. I saw Susan before and she said that Joan said that Tommy said. . . ."

"Tracy, get to the point," Jen said with exasperation.

"I *am*. Susan said that Tommy saw Mia going into the nurse's office this morning. I guess she wasn't feeling well."

Nora finished her sandwich and stood

up. "I'm going to go and see what's with her. After all, maybe I can help."

Jen said, "I'll go with you. But I think Mrs. Haggerty can take care of things herself."

"Mrs. Haggerty is only a nurse, Jen. And I have been working in a doctor's office."

"One day," Steve said. "Just one day, Nora."

Nora ignored them and said to Jen, "Are you coming or not?"

"I'm coming, I'm coming. Relax."

"Every minute counts in illness, Jen. You should know that."

In the nurse's office, Mia was lying on a cot, covered to her chin with a blanket. Jen got frightened when she saw how pale Mia looked. She walked to the cot and bent over. "Mia, what's wrong?"

Mia looked away and mumbled, "I don't feel well." She pulled the blanket up until it covered the lower part of her face.

Nora took a hold of the blanket and gave it a pull. "Mia, it's warm in here. You don't need a blanket over your face."

The blanket slid down and Mia pulled the raincoat she had on up as high as she could. "Go away," she whispered.

Jen looked at the raincoat and asked, "Why are you wearing my coat? I mean

115

it's okay with me, but I never thought you'd want to wear a plain old raincoat."

Mia looked at Jen and winced. "I don't want to wear any of your clothes. They're awful."

"Gee, thanks, Mia," Jen said.

"I don't mean that. I mean they are okay for you but not for me."

"So who said they were right for you?" Nora asked.

Suddenly, Mia stood up, took off the raincoat, and stood there in Jen's navy skirt, frilly blouse, and pumps. "Jeff said so."

Jen and Nora looked at Mia and both burst out laughing at the same time.

Mia turned away and said angrily, "You don't have to laugh. I feel bad enough. How can I let anyone see me looking like this? But I can't go home. Not to Jen's home, not to mine. I have nowhere to go."

Nora sat down on the cot and thought for a minute. "Okay, this is what you do. Everyone knows you went to Mrs. Haggerty's office. Okay? So you say she said you seem okay to her, but she said to keep nice and warm today so you don't get a chill or something. Then you just keep on Jen's raincoat, buttoned up high, all day."

Jen agreed. "And you have to tell Jeff not to do that anymore. That you have to be allowed to dress the way you want. Even if you look. . . ."

"Look *how*?" Mia asked belligerently.

"Fine. Just fine," Jen said graciously. "Come on. We're all going to be late for class. Just button up the coat and keep it on."

In English class, Mia sat huddled in her coat, but everyone accepted her explanation. Steve went over to Mia after class and said, "You look funny in that coat, Mia. Why don't you ask Denise how to look, well, good . . . you know."

That should impress Denise, Steve thought. Everyone likes a compliment. That's a pretty debonair thing to say.

Denise groaned. "You don't think I would want Mia to dress like I do, do you? We are totally different types. Can't you see that?"

Jen looked at Steve with disdain and said, "That is *my* raincoat Mia is wearing. So *what* is so funny about it?"

Steve gazed at Denise and then Jen and walked away, shaking his head. Mr. Ryder may have advised Tommy okay, he thought, but he sure is messing up with me.

At the end of the day, Jason followed the instructions Mike had given him. He went into the boys' room and changed into a pair of running shorts and a sweatshirt. He put a band around his bright red hair and looked in the mirror. He shuddered at his long, skinny legs and the red hair pushed up into spikes by the band. But he'd promised Mike. Looking out of the boys' room door, he made sure the corridor was empty and then ran outside the building, where Mike was waiting for him. Mike had on shorts, too. How come I don't look like him? Jason thought.

"Okay," Mike said, as Jason approached him. "We'll start out easy. Three miles."

"Three miles?" Jason shouted. "I'll die."

"Don't be a wimp, Jason. Three miles is nothing. Start running."

As they ran through the streets, Jason puffed noisily. When they got to Temptations, he knew he had been right and he was going to die. *Everyone* was standing in front of the ice-cream parlor. And they were all looking at him.

"Hey, Jason," Tommy yelled. "Do a mile for me."

Mitch laughed loudly. "Mike, you don't know what you're doing. He's probably never run a block."

Jen and Lucy tried not to laugh, but it was hard. "He looks so funny," Lucy whispered in Jen's ear.

Tracy just stared and then she said, "I didn't know you were supposed to look like that in running shorts. I thought. . . . "

"Whatever you thought, you were right, Tracy," Lucy said.

"For once," Tracy said.

Jason turned to say something to the group and slipped. His feet flew off the ground and he landed with a thud. Mike looked over his shoulder and yelled, "Up an' at 'em, Jas-boy. Just keep going."

Jason stood up, brushed off his shorts, and trotted after Mike. Maybe I'm not cut out for *any* sport, he thought.

Nora went to Dr. Armanson's office right after school. It was the afternoon Dr. Armanson volunteered at the clinic at the hospital, so all Nora had to do was answer the phone and type up the month's bills. She was almost dozing off when the phone rang, making her jump.

"I'd like to speak to Dr. Armanson. This is Ms. Manlow."

Nora cleared her throat and said in what she felt was her grown-up voice, the one she tried to use with all Dr. Armanson's patients, "I'm sorry, Ms. Manlow, but the doctor is at the hospital this afternoon and won't have any office hours. I'll take a message."

"Oh," Ms. Manlow said, sounding very disappointed. "I just have had this pain in the back of my legs for a few days . . . too much exercise class, you know. I always think I can do more than I can. Look, I'll talk to the doctor tomorrow. It's nothing that can't wait."

Nora knew what too much exercise could do. "Why don't you just take an aspirin?" Nora said. "That should help."

"What a dope I am," Ms. Manlow said. "I never even thought of that. Thanks."

Nora sat at the desk, feeling great pleasure. She had helped a patient. She was certainly on the way to being a good doctor.

At five-thirty, she did what Dr. Armanson had told her to do. She put all the messages in an envelope and brought them home with her. When Dr. Armanson came home, she handed them to him and he went through them all. "Okay, Nora, there are just a few people I have to call back tonight. The rest can wait until tomorrow. Anything else happen in the office?"

Nora could hardly wait to tell him. "Well, Ms. Manlow called. The back of her legs were bothering her from over-exercising, so I just told her to take an aspirin."

Dr. Armanson looked at Nora for a long moment. "You did what?" he asked.

"I told her to take an aspirin," Nora repeated proudly.

"*You* prescribed medication to a patient of mine?" His voice rose, filled with anger.

"I didn't prescribe medication," Nora said. "I told her take a harmless aspirin."

Dr. Armanson walked to Nora and gazed at her with cold, worried eyes. "There is no such thing as a harmless aspirin. How do you know she wasn't allergic to it? How do you know she didn't have something wrong with her that aspirin would have been all wrong for? How do you know that aspirin wouldn't mask other symptoms I'd want to be aware of? What made you think you were able to give any advice to anyone?"

"I didn't think. . . ." Nora's voice shook and her eyes filled with tears.

"Right, Nora, you didn't think. I won't need you at the office tomorrow, Nora," Dr. Armanson said. "I think you have a little maturing to do before you should be 'around a doctor's office."

The Armansons and Nora sat around the dinner table that night in silence. Lucy's mother said, "Harvey, she didn't mean any harm. . . ."

"I know that, Liz. I know Nora is a good, caring girl, but she could have done harm."

"Did I?" Nora asked in a low voice, "Did I hurt her?"

"No, Nora. I'm sure you didn't. Helen Manlow does this all the time. But that isn't what this is about. This is about understanding what your capabilities and responsibilities are. You have to learn that."

Nora went up to her room after dinner and cried quietly against a yellow pillow. When she stopped, she called Jen.

"I've made a mess of everything," she said, beginning to cry again. Quietly, she explained to Jen.

"Oh, Nora, you meant well. And you didn't hurt her. So. . . ."

Nora shook her head. "He was right, Jen. I was stupid."

Jen was silent and then she said, "Okay, so you were stupid. We're just kids, you know. We all do stupid things. But you learned, didn't you?"

"I guess," Nora said. "But why is learning something always hard? Why can't it be easy?"

Chapter 12

At breakfast on Friday morning, Barbara Hendrix said to Jen, "What do you want to serve tomorrow night and how many do you want to invite?"

Jen shrugged. "I don't care what we eat, really. You can decide that. Jeff used to make a pot of chili or something. And I guess I'll just ask the regular bunch." I'd like to leave Steve out, she thought. But she knew she wouldn't.

Then Jen turned to Tony, who was in his usual morning mood . . . sullen. "Tony, you'll come, too, won't you?"

Tony looked up from his orange juice and smiled in a strange way. "Jen, I'm not going to a party with a bunch of kids. I've got better things to do." He got up and poured a cup of coffee from an electric pot on the buffet and left the room.

Jen sat in silence, her cheeks burning, tears forming in her eyes. Okay, so he thought she was a baby, but he could have refused in a nicer way. Actually, *he* was the baby for not being able to act in a more mature fashion, she thought.

Mr. Hendrix folded his paper and stood up. "Barbara, you have to do something about him. He is impossible in the mornings."

"What do you mean *I* have to do something about him?" Barbara Hendrix said. "He's your son, too."

Mr. Hendrix left, mumbling to himself about rude children.

Mrs. Hendrix reached over and patted Jen's hand. "Don't pay any attention to Tony, Jen, dear. Anyway, you have a nice boyfriend, don't you? I remember Denise saying something about it."

Jen wiped her eyes. "I think my nice boyfriend thinks Denise would make a nice girlfriend. I don't seem to be having much luck with boys these days."

Barbara Hendrix frowned. "You mean Denise is flirting with *your* boyfriend?"

Jen shook her head. "It's more the other way around."

Jen and Nora huddled next to each other on the bus, each deep in her own sad thoughts. Finally Jen said, "I think I'm through with men."

Nora nodded. "I think I'm through with being a doctor."

"We could join the Peace Corps together," Jen said. "And go off to some faraway place no one has ever heard of."

"If no one has ever heard of it, how did the Peace Corps find out it existed?" Nora asked.

"Oh, get lost!" Jen said.

On the steps of the school, Steve walked over to Denise as soon as he saw Jen coming up the path. He bowed to Denise and handed her a dying daisy he had found near a garbage can. "For you," he said.

Denise looked at the flower, took it, walked over to a pail near the school, and threw the daisy in it. "Don't ever give me a dead flower again, Steve. Is that all you think I'm worth?"

Denise started to walk away from Steve, but then she turned back. "Anyway, what is going on? Why are you always hanging around me, acting goofy? Don't bother me anymore. I thought you were Jen's boyfriend. Go bother her and give her dead daisies."

She sharply turned away from Steve. As she did, her long blonde hair swung and slapped Steve in the face.

Even her hair doesn't like me, Steve thought. But she's right and Mr. Ryder is wrong. It's Jen I want to be with. He walked down a few steps to where Jen was standing, inviting the class to her party.

"Jen," he said softly. Then he didn't know what else to say. Finally he stammered, "What's new?"

Jen glared at Steve and said angrily, "What's new is that you are being a dork over Denise. But if that's the kind of boy you are: unreliable, fickle, dumb, that's all right with me. Who needs you?"

Jen started to walk away, but Steve grabbed her arm. "Let me explain. It's all Mr. Ryder's fault. He — "

Jen interrupted Steve. "Now you are asking me to believe it was all Mr. Ryder's fault? You must think I'm a real jerk, with no common sense at all." This time she stalked away, leaving Steve staring after her sadly.

Denise invited all the girls to her house, to Mia's house really, after school. "I need moral support," she said. "I also need someone to show me how to clean the bathroom."

They all sprawled around the living room, eating potato chips and drinking soft drinks, much to Nora's disgust. Lucy kept looking at her watch, until Tracy asked, "Have you got a date or something, Lucy?"

Lucy shook her head no. "There are other reasons for looking at one's watch,

Tracy, than having a date with some boy. I have much bigger problems than that."

"I can't think of any better reason to look at a watch than because you're meeting a boy," Tracy said, looking at Lucy with a puzzled expression.

"You're hopeless, Tracy," Nora said. "You live in a time of great opportunities for women and all you can think of is boys."

Now Tracy looked hurt. "Everyone doesn't want to be a doctor like you do."

"That was yesterday," Nora mumbled.

Lucy looked at her watch again and Jen asked, "What is with you, Lucy? What's the watch business for?"

"It's Mrs. Crowley. She's got this thing about me getting home before the traffic gets 'heavy,' as she calls it. Did you ever see heavy traffic in Cedar Groves, except maybe during Christmas shopping time?" Lucy straightened the straps of her denim overalls and stood up. "I'd better go or she'll call out the police."

Jen took a bite of an apple and said thoughtfully, "It's funny but she isn't like that with Steve. She just lets him do his thing."

Lucy shrugged. "Maybe she doesn't care if Steve gets run over. And neither should you, Jen . . . the way he's been carrying on over Denise. It's disgusting."

Denise made a face in agreement.

Jen reached for a potato chip. "I don't want Steve to get run over . . . not really. I just wish he'd move away so I never have to see him again."

"Look, Jen," Nora said. "He isn't going to move away so you just have to be the mature one and ignore him. Find another boy."

Denise tied back her long hair into a ponytail with a red ribbon and said, "Enough of this boy talk. Someone has to show me how to clean a bathroom. It's my job for tomorrow and I have to show Mia's mother that I'm not a dork. So what do I do first?"

Mia looked at Denise and grinned. "I don't believe you. You really don't know how to clean up a bathroom?"

"Even *I* know that," Tracy said.

"So come on and show me," Denise said impatiently.

"Denise," Nora said. "No one should have to show you. You simply wash the floor, clean the sink, tub, and john. . . ."

Denise made a gagging sound. "Yuck."

Nora ignored her and went on, "You polish all the silver stuff and the mirror, and there you are with a clean bathroom. Now, I have to go. Dr. Armanson is probably waiting to lecture me a little more."

"I have to go, too," Jen said. "I'll see you all tomorrow night. Seven-thirtyish."

Denise walked them all to the door and said, "Rats deserting a sinking ship. That's what you all are."

Mia patted her on her shoulders. "Don't worry. My mother isn't such a good bathroom-cleaner herself. Anyway, one more day and then you can go back to being a princess. You'll survive."

"I'm not so sure," Denise said.

When Lucy got home, Mrs. Crowley was peering out of the living room window with a frown on her face. "I was beginning to get worried," she said.

Now or never, Lucy thought. "Mrs. Crowley, what's going on? Jen said you don't get frantic about Steve. You don't have crazy curfews for him. So why me?"

Carol Crowley looked surprised. "Of course I'm not on Steve's back the way I am on yours. He's a boy."

Lucy sank down into a big, brown easy chair. "What has *that* got to do with it?"

Mrs. Crowley sat on the sofa next to Lucy's chair. "I've never had a daughter . . . never been responsible for a girl before. I just feel girls need more watching after. Girls make me nervous."

Lucy burst out laughing. "Mrs. Crowley,

girls aren't any more likely to get hit by a car after dark than boys. Really, we aren't made of glass. Have you been miserable the whole time I've been here? I mean, worried and nervous and unhappy?"

Mrs. Crowley grabbed Lucy's hands. "No! No, of course not. I've loved having you. I just have to learn to deal with you the same way I deal with Steve. Almost, anyway. I guess I must seem so old-fashioned to you. I'll learn. You'll see."

Lucy squeezed Carol Crowley's hands. "I go home day after tomorrow, you know. You're going to have to learn fast. Like tomorrow night, Jen is having a party at Denise's house. You have to promise not to worry about what time I'm going to get home. Give me a reasonable curfew and I'll live up to it."

Mrs. Crowley grinned. "Nine o'clock?"

"A little later than that," Lucy said, grinning back. Then she looked down at the floor. "You know, I've learned something from you, too."

"What is that?" Carol Crowley asked.

"Well, I heard you were the most intellectual woman in Cedar Groves. You know, always taking courses and stuff, and I thought you would be hard to talk to. Instead, you're just like all mothers . . . a worrier."

"You mean, I'm not so smart after all."

"That's not exactly what I meant. It's just I was worried, too, and I didn't have to be. We didn't talk about Egyptian flowers once."

Chapter 13

Nora sat in silence at the Armansons' dinner table. They talked about what they had done during the day, what was going on in Washington, the conversation Mrs. Armanson had had with Lucy that day, but Nora didn't say a word.

Finally she asked Dr. Armanson, "How were things in the office today?"

"Everything was all right. Mary was feeling much better and came in."

"I'm glad," Nora said softly.

Dr. Armanson peered at her from under his bushy eyebrows. "Of course, she doesn't come in on Saturday and I have office hours from noon until three."

Nora nodded.

Dr. Armanson busily cut the chicken on his plate. "Would you like to help out again, Nora? I could use you tomorrow."

A wide grin spread over Nora's face. "Do you mean it? Really?"

"I'm asking you, aren't I?" Harvey Armanson said. "Although I know there is a party for you kids tomorrow night. You may have things to do during the day. When Lucy is going out at night she spends half the afternoon polishing her nails, and washing her hair, and trying on clothes."

"No. No," Nora said. "I'd much rather be in your office. Thank you so much."

She jumped out of her chair and ran over to Dr. Armanson. She bent over and kissed his cheek. "You trust me?"

He laughed. "I think you learned something the other day."

"I did. I'll *never* prescribe medicine again as long as I live."

Dr. Armanson patted Nora's cheek. "Not that long. When you have an MD after your name you can prescribe the proper medication. Just wait until then."

Nora went back to her seat and hungrily began to eat the food on her plate that a few moments before hadn't interested her at all. Dr. Armanson watched her and said with sincerity, "You're going to make it, Nora. I have a gut feeling about you."

The Hillards had finished dinner. Mrs. Hillard, knowing that Tracy would be so busy getting ready for the party that Saturday's dinner would be unimportant, had made a special meal on Friday. As a result, the kitchen was filled with dirty pots and dishes. After he drank the last bit of coffee in his cup, Mr. Hillard patted his stomach and got up from the table. "That was a delicious meal, Eve. Really good."

Eve Hillard beamed. "Thank you, Sam. I'm glad you liked it."

Sam Hillard kissed his wife's cheek. "I'll just go into the living room and catch up on the evening paper."

Tracy watched him walk away from the table crammed with dirty dishes. She turned to Mrs. Hillard and said, "What would Susan do if Mr. Hillard just walked away from the table like that without helping at all?"

Eve Hillard thought for a moment and then answered. "Why, Susan does just what he does. After dinner she watches television, or does her homework, or reads."

"You mean *she* doesn't help, either?" Tracy asked.

"I guess not," Mrs. Hillard said. "But it's all right because. . . ."

"No, it isn't all right," Tracy interrupted. "Mrs. Hillard, I realized something. You and I are a lot alike. We both let people take advantage of us. And that's wrong."

"Well . . . I guess what you say is true, but I've been doing it so long I just wouldn't know how to change."

Tracy took a deep breath. "Believe it or not, Mrs. Hillard, I'm doing this as much for me as for you. Now, this is what you do. You go into Mr. Hillard and you say to him, " 'Mr. Hillard, please clear the table. I've worked hard making this wonderful dinner and now I'd like you to help me clean up.' *That's* what you do."

"I don't know, Tracy," Eve Hillard said. "I've never asked him before to help me."

"I know I'm interfering and maybe I shouldn't," Tracy said. "But people like you and me have to help each other. I'll be right with . . . behind . . . you."

Slowly, Mrs. Hillard walked into the living room. "Mr. Hillard," she said, "please clear the table. I've worked hard making this wonderful dinner and now I'd like you to help me clean up."

Sam Hillard looked up from his paper with surprise. "What is this 'Mr. Hillard' bit? Since when are we so formal with each other?"

"I'm sorry," Mrs. Hillard said. "I meant, Sam, please clear the table."

He stood up and put the paper on the seat of the chair. "Sure. You never asked before, so I just thought you didn't want any help."

Mrs. Hillard turned to Tracy and just stared. Tracy took her arm and they went back into the kitchen. Mr. Hillard came in with a pile of dishes and said, "You know, Susan could help a little around here, too. That girl doesn't do a thing. You have to speak up, Eve. Speak up."

You could have offered to help, Tracy thought, but she didn't say anything. Things were going too well.

Dinner was over at the Pauleys', too. Mike grabbed Jason's arm and said, "Come on, there's a great football game on TV. I'll explain every move to you, so we can practice them tomorrow. Or would you rather run again?"

Jason thought about the way he looked in running shorts and said, "No, football will be great. Just great."

He followed Mike into the den and tried to look forward to a night of football. Just tonight, he thought. Tomorrow night was the party and the next night he would be home. And he could oil his skateboard wheels.

Mia was up in Jen's room, trying to figure out what to wear the next night, when Jeff came in. He looked at the all-black outfit Mia had laid out on the bed. Black sweater, black skirt, black tights, and black shoes. A bottle of black nail polish was on the bureau.

"Mia, don't you think you'd look good in something a little brighter?" Jeff asked.

"I don't think so, Jeff," Mia said.

"Well, why don't you just try a little scarf or. . . ."

"Jeff," Mia said, as she put the black polish on her nails, "Jen said that I have to tell you that I have to be allowed to dress the way I want. So . . . Jeff . . . I'm going to wear all this black stuff tomorrow night."

Jeff looked hurt. "Jen said that?"

"She said it very nicely," Mia added hastily, "but she did say it."

Jeff sat down on the bed and watched Mia putting the polish on. "Jen really said that?"

"Hmmm," Mia replied. "She really did."

"Imagine that," Jeff said with a puzzled tone to his voice.

He looked as if his world were falling into little pieces. "I tell you what, Jeff," Mia said thoughtfully. "Supposing I wash the orange color out of my hair. That would be easy to do. And I'll just put a nice very light pink in. Would that make you happier?"

Jeff threw his head back and laughed . . . loud. He hugged Mia, careful not to smudge her black polish. "Mia, you *are* a nice girl. And I think a very light pink color in your hair would be gorgeous . . . simply gorgeous. Tell Jen I said so."

"Well, Stevie-boy, how is it going with your girlfriend?" Mr. Ryder asked as he and Steve stacked the dishes in the dishwasher. "Has my advice paid off?"

It sure has, Steve thought. Now neither Denise nor Jen want anything to do with me. Sometimes adults just don't understand how kids operate. He was about to tell Mr. Ryder that his advice not only hadn't paid off but it had gotten him into more trouble than he knew how to deal with. But he looked at Bob Ryder's eager face, at the interest in his eyes, and he decided to let it go. After all, Mr. Ryder hadn't meant any harm. And it did seem to work for Tommy. But then Steve thought about Tommy. Tommy was one of those guys who *thought* every girl liked him, and every girl did like him, for a while. But sooner or later they all realized Tommy was just a lightweight, a guy who just had to charm every girl he met. And sooner or later the girls decided they didn't want to be one of a mob.

Steve smiled at Bob Ryder, "Everything's fine, Mr. Ryder. Just fine."

Yeah, Steve thought, just fine. But fine for who? Certainly not him. And Jen didn't look too happy, either. And Denise thought he was a jerk. Great!

The next morning, Denise was in the bathroom at six o'clock. Mrs. Stevens had told her that she slept late on Saturday mornings, so Denise had plenty of time. She rolled the sleeves of her satin pajamas up, pinned back her hair, put on a pair of rubber gloves that were in the kitchen, and looked around. In her mind she went over what Nora had said. Wash the floor, clean the sink, tub, and john, polish the faucets, and she was done. But what Nora hadn't told her was the order of action. So Denise washed the floor first, and by the time she had cleaned the sink and tub, the floor was dirty again. Her fingermarks were all over the white tile, the faucets had globs of cleanser stuck to them, and the mirror kept fogging up.

Denise's hair came loose from the barrettes and hung in her eyes; her sleeves kept slipping down and dipping into the pail of water she had; and the legs of her pajamas were soaking wet. She sat back on her heels on the floor and felt like screaming, but she narrowed her lips and started again. At nine o'clock, she surveyed what she had done. It was perfect. Everything was shining. Everything was clean. Denise smiled and decided that she had never felt as proud of herself as she did that moment.

She went back into her room, took off her sopping pajamas, put on a clean pair, and got back into bed. Within two minutes she was asleep. A loud banging on the door woke her an hour later.

The door flew open and Mrs. Stevens stood there. "Denise, it is ten o'clock. We just don't sleep all day here. Come on, get up. You have things to do today. The bathroom among them."

Denise raised herself on one elbow and smiled at Dana Stevens. "Why don't you shower first and then I will."

"Okay, but get yourself out of bed *now*." Mrs. Stevens walked out of the room and Denise heard her going into the bathroom. A minute later she was back. "What did you do . . . stay up all night?"

"Six o'clock this morning," Denise answered proudly.

Dana Stevens sat down on the bed and hugged Denise. "It's perfect. Cleaner than I ever get it." Suddenly she looked at Denise suspiciously. "You didn't get your maid to come over here during the night? Did you?"

"No!" Denise shouted. "I did that bathroom all by myself. Then, I was kind of tired, so I went back to bed for a little while."

Mrs. Stevens looked like she could hardly keep from laughing. "How long did it take you? To do the bathroom, I mean?"

Denise didn't want to tell her but she did. "Three hours."

Mia's mother stood up and pulled Denise with her. "Come on. I'm going to make you the biggest, best breakfast you have ever had. *And* I am going to do all the cleaning up, too. You will be *my* guest this morning."

Denise stood in the middle of the room, her long blonde hair hanging over her bright blue eyes. "I did good, didn't I?" she asked shyly.

"You did wonderfully, Denise. If you ever have to, you can always get a job as a bathroom cleaner." Mrs. Stevens lovingly pushed Denise to the door.

Jen sat at the breakfast table with Barbara Hendrix, going over what they would have to eat at the party. She kept looking at the door, waiting for Tony to come in. "He's out playing tennis, Jen," Mrs. Hendrix said.

"Oh," Jen answered, not trying to pretend she hadn't been looking for Tony. "I don't know why I even care. He thinks I'm just a kid. And Steve . . . well, he . . . he's just been so peculiar lately. He even blames his dumb behavior on Mr. Ryder."

"What has Bob Ryder got to do with anything?" Mrs. Hendrix asked.

Jen shrugged. "I don't know. Boys are strange sometimes."

"Men, too," Denise's mother said.

Chapter 14

By eight o'clock Saturday night, the den at Denise's house was filled. The music was loud; the laughter was loud. A large table at the side of the room was covered with food, and there was a big group of people around it already. Jen stood to one side and watched everyone having a good time . . . everyone but her. She felt like an outsider, and all she wanted to do was go home and crawl into her father's lap and have him comfort her. Funny, she thought, I don't think of crawling into Mrs. Hendrix's lap. I loved being with her, but it's my dad I want when I'm feeling unhappy. I guess my dad is my mother, too . . . a little.

Suddenly, a hand was in front of her, holding a glass of soda. "Want some?" Steve stood next to her, with a cautious expression in his blue eyes.

Jen pushed his hand away. "I don't want anything from you. Go find Denise."

"I don't want Denise, Jen. I never did. That's what I've been trying to tell you."

Jen snorted. "You sure *seemed* to want Denise."

Steve put the soda down on a table and put his hand on Jen's arm. "Please, you have to listen to me." He took Jen's hand and led her outside. The air was cold, but they sat down on a glider on the slate patio. He took off his jacket and put it around Jen's shoulders.

"Like I said . . . it was Mr. Ryder's idea. He said if I pretended to be interested in some other girl, you would be more interested in *me*. And I figured, well, Tommy was such a success with girls, and he must have gotten his information from his father, so I thought I'd just do what Mr. Ryder said. But I never really *liked* Denise."

Jen was silent. Then she said, "You know, this doesn't make any sense. I already was 'interested' in you, as Mr. Ryder put it. So why did you have to go through all that dumb pretending? I mean, if a person likes a person then they like a person."

"I guess I wasn't sure, Jen. So I just did what I did."

Jen looked into Steve's eyes. He was really such an honest boy, she knew that, and he looked so miserable at that moment that she couldn't stay mad at him. "Promise me something, Steve."

"Anything," Steve said fervently.

"Don't ever listen to Mr. Ryder . . . or Tommy again."

"I promise," Steve said. "You're not mad anymore?"

Jen laughed. "No."

Steve bent over and kissed Jen. His mouth was warm in the cool air. Jen put her head on his shoulder and felt happy again. So what if Steve is a little stupid when it comes to girls, she thought. Then she lifted her head and said, "One more thing — you have to tell Denise about this so she understands, too."

Steve heaved a huge sigh. "She's going to think I'm crazy."

"She thinks you're crazy as it is," Jen said. "This can't make things any worse."

Steve said, "Okay. I'll do it." Then he pulled Jen up from the swing. "You look cold. Let's go back in."

Inside, Jason was staring at Mia. "You look like you're going to a funeral," he said.

Mia smoothed the black sweater over her shoulders. "You don't know anything about style, Jason."

"I know that pink hair is not for human beings," Jason said. "I think the orange was better."

145

Mia looked concerned. "Do you really think so?"

"What do I know?" Jason answered.

"You sure don't know enough not to be seen in public in running shorts," Mia said, as Nora came over to them.

"Jason," Nora said, "I saw a skateboard in the hall closet when I hung up my coat. I'm sure it isn't Denise's or Tony's, so it must be yours. I thought you had given it up for track or football or basketball or something."

Jason blushed slightly. "I gave all that up. I just don't want to put the other guys on the teams to shame. You know, show them up as amateurs in the face of my expertise. So I'm back with the skateboard."

"What a loss that will be to Cedar Groves Junior High," Mia said.

"Well, it's all for the best. I told Mike tonight that he better find some kid who *really* needs help and devote himself to him. I'm going to be generous and let Mike go. Actually, I was teaching *him* more then he was teaching *me*. I just pretend to be awkward. You know."

"We know," Mia and Nora said together.

At ten o'clock, Denise peered out of the window and said, "There's a car coming up the driveway. Everyone you invited is here, aren't they, Jen?"

"I think so," Jen answered, looking around the room.

"Hey, Lucy, maybe it's Mrs. Crowley coming to get you and bring you home," Nora teased.

"No way," Lucy said. "Mrs. Crowley and I have come to an understanding. I have a twelve o'clock curfew and she promised not to start biting her nails until twelve-thirty."

In a few minutes, Tony came into the room. He walked over to Jen and looked down at her. "Mind if I join the party for a little while?"

Jen twisted a gold bracelet around her wrist and then said to Tony, "I thought you didn't go to kids' parties."

Tony reached for Jen's hand. "I'm sorry, Jen. I'm pretty grouchy in the mornings. But we're friends. You were such a help to me when I broke up with Jessica Hartnett. You were so kind and considerate. Remember?"

"I remember, Tony. But I didn't think you did."

"I do. I just forget *sometimes*. Look, would you dance with me?"

Jen nodded and moved to the area where the rugs had been taken away and everyone was dancing. She saw Steve at the food table, a fork in his hand halfway to his mouth. He looked surprised and worried. Let him have a taste of his own medicine, Jen thought. And then . . . No, that would make me as bad as he's been. He may have been a turkey, but I'm not.

Jen walked over to Steve and said, "You know Tony Hendrix, Denise's brother. You know we're good friends. I think."

"Sure. Hi, Hendrix."

Tony saw the suspicious look in Steve's eyes and smiled. "One dance with Jen and then I have to go out. Okay?"

Steve let out a breath. "Fine. Fine. Glad you're going. I mean, glad you're here."

"Sure," Tony said.

At eleven-thirty, Mrs. Hendrix came into the den and rang a silver bell she had in her hand. Everyone turned to listen to her. "I just want to say, I hope you all had a good time. I know that tomorrow morning all of you will go back to your real homes. I know your parents will be glad to have you back, and I hope you all enjoyed being in your new homes as much as I enjoyed having Jen here. Okay, kids, half an hour more and then this party is officially over."

At twelve, everyone milled around, yelling, "See you Monday." "Talk to you to-morrow." "Bet your foster parents will be glad to get rid of you." "Bet your real parents won't be so happy to see you."

Then they all left.

When Jen was in bed, Barbara Hendrix came into her room. "I meant what I said, Jen. I loved having you here . . . *and* your ducky pajamas. I just want you to know, if you ever want an older woman to talk to or to ask advice of or anything, I'm here. You'll remember that, won't you?

Jen kissed Denise's mother's cheek and lay back against the pillows. "It's been wonderful, Mrs. Hendrix. I'm going to miss you . . . and Denise's bathroom."

Chapter 15

On Sunday night, Jen was snuggled down in her own bed in her own room in her own home, when the phone rang. She knew it would be Nora.

"How does it feel to be home?" Nora asked.

"It's good," Jen replied. "I liked being at Denise's and I love Mrs. Hendrix, but there's no place like home, as they say."

"Me, too," Nora said. "I learned a lot at the Armansons', but I'm glad to be home. It's more relaxing. You don't always have to be on your best behavior."

After Jen hung up, her father came into her room. He sat down on the edge of her bed and took her hand. "I can't tell you how much I missed you. Jeff, too, and even Eric. I don't know what I'll do when you go off to college."

Jen put her head on her father's shoulder. "Let's not think about that yet."

"Was it good for you . . . at the Hendrixes,' I mean," Ted Mann asked. "Did you learn anything you didn't already know?"

Jen smiled. "I learned that you don't have to be a woman to be good at mothering. You do good at both, Dad, mothering *and* fathering."

In the social studies class on Monday morning, the members of the Eighth Grade Switch talked loudly to each other until Ms. Dalton came into the room. She had a wide grin on her face as she perched on the edge of her desk.

"Okay," she said, "I can hardly wait. I want each of you to tell me one thing you learned this past week. We'll start with you, Denise."

Denise stood up and said proudly. "I am probably the best bathroom cleaner in the whole city. And I'm proud of it."

Nora stood up next. "I know not to take more responsibility on myself than I'm ready for. I also know, I *am* going to be a doctor, without a doubt."

Jen didn't get up, but she spoke out. "Even nice people can be terrible grouches sometimes . . . and you just have to accept that."

Mia thought for a minute and then said, "It's not so bad to compromise . . . a little."

Jason held up his skateboard and said, "This is the only sport I want to be involved in."

Tracy said, "Like mother, like daughter isn't necessarily so."

Steve looked at Jen and said, "You have to be honest with the people you like and not play games."

Lucy smiled, thinking of Mrs. Crowley. "Sometimes a kid can teach an adult something pretty important."

Ms. Dalton looked around the room and said, "You did better than I thought you would. You really did learn important things. Okay. Anyone sorry to be home?"

"No!" came the shout. Everyone seemed to agree on that.

"Anyone want to do this switch thing again?"

"Maybe in ten years," Nora said. "Not before."

"Anybody still bored with their own life?" the teacher asked.

"Not at the moment," Steve said.

"Give us a little more time," Denise said.

"Okay," Ms. Dalton said. "Your paper on this last week is due in two weeks."

A groan went up from the class.

After school, Nora and Jen walked home together. "It's good to be doing this, and to know what to expect when we get home," Jen said. "Even the same old food is good."

"Jeff should hear you call his dinners 'the same old food.' "

"You know what I mean," Jen said.

Nora nodded. "I know."

"I'll call you tonight," Jen said when they got to her house. "Do you want to come in for a little while?"

Nora hesitated. "I don't think so. I think I'll just go right home and pester Sally a little."

"Me, too," Jen said. "I mean I'll pester Eric and Jeff . . . just like old times. I guess old times can be good times."

"Sometimes." Nora said.

"A lot of times," Jen added.

"This time you're right," Nora said.

Is Cedar Groves the next prize-winning model school? Not if the eighth grade has anything to do with it! Read Junior High #12, THE REVOLT OF THE EIGHTH GRADE.

The Girls of Canby Hall®

by Emily Chase

School pressures! Boy trouble! Roommate rivalry! The girls of Canby Hall are learning about life and love now that they've left home to live in a private boarding school.